Nobby's Diary

I. R. Walker

CONTENTS

AUTHOR'S NOTE

Although this book is a work of fiction, it draws from real events that occurred in mid-1980's Britain.

Fleet Street printing presses warmed the homeless; the GPO Tower was empty, as were the Docklands. Centerpoint was London's biggest white elephant; newspapers were relocating to the Darkness on the Edge of Town and the BBC was rumoured to have thrown out perfectly good cameras so they could shoot their soap opera on sparkly, new equipment.

To discover more, visit NobbysDiary.com

1. AN ILL WIND

McKenzie was not happy.

"Not another Christmas party!" he seethed through gritted teeth.

"Never volunteer for anything; never cause a commotion; always keep your nose clean and your head down" Wasn't that what his dad had taught him? And his grandad before that! Of course, while all the staff muckety-mucks were upstairs eating and drinking themselves into a stupor at the office party, here he was in the basement--sleeves rolled up, elbows raw, eyes strained -- taking stock of all the ancient printing equipment. Of course, the newspaper just had to relocate over the holidays--and he was the one who had to take the inventory.

"Can't say I'll be sorry to see the back of all this junk," he murmured as he surveyed the dingy basement and erased another item from his clipboard.

McKenzie puttered around the windowless machine room. He could hear the hubbub of conversation and clinking glasses tumbling down from the party upstairs, mingling with the drone of passing Fleet Street traffic. Eventually, enough was enough.

"I need a drink!" he said to himself. He dropped his clipboard, threw his frayed raincoat over his arm and vaulted up the stairs, slamming the door behind him.

If only McKenzie had stayed a few moments longer, he might have nipped in the bud the following sequence of events: If only ... he had stopped to fill out the required Machine Service & Maintenance Form A303B-Pt2 he might have heard the squeak of a rusty bolt loosened from its nut. If only... he had lingered to try to catch fragments of gossip from the office party upstairs, he might

1

have heard the hacking cough coming from inside the huge piece of machinery behind him. If only… he had returned for his keys, he might have seen a pair of rheumy eyes framed in the glare of a weak flashlight or the gnarled fingers that retrieved a couple of screws that had fallen onto the oil-stained floor. If only. None of that happened, though. The pub was calling and McKenzie needed a drink.

Later that evening, he cast a lonely figure as he left The Olde Bell Tavern. Wrapped in his shabby coat, McKenzie pushed onwards against the bitter wind that swept along the Thames, over Blackfriars Bridge and down the Embankment. He stepped around the vagrants who slept on the side streets, trying to stay away from the harshest blasts of cold air.

Only the homeless, the foolish or the drunk should be out in this weather, he thought, and — in his inebriated state — not even recognizing that he qualified for two out of three.

"Any change, mate?"

McKenzie peered into the storm and into the craggy and careworn face of a homeless man who held out a calloused palm.

"Change in what?" After a couple of foggy seconds, McKenzie understood. "Ah, money… Sorry, no," he mumbled and moved away. No way was he taking his hands out of his pockets on a night like this.

As McKenzie continued along the Embankment, the wind picked up strength. It whirled and whistled around his head and was soon accompanied by driving rain. It scattered the pages of discarded newspapers and sent them diving and dancing along the street, almost as if they had a life of their own. McKenzie -- his shoulders hunched and drawn -- fought his way through the storm and the newspapers that continued to torment him.

***

Harry Sweetnum was not happy, either. Having left work at The Scribe, he took a packed Northern Line train home. It took him 10 minutes to walk past the gray, characterless streets to his gray, characterless, semi-detached home. He was soaked. Fumbling for his keys, he opened the front door and tossed the remnants of his cheap umbrella onto the floor. He glanced into the kitchen and saw his wife — Denise — peeling potatoes at the sink and his son —

Spencer — sitting at the table. Without acknowledging either, he walked into the dining room and poured himself a drink from that awful, faux crystal decanter that was an anniversary gift from the in-laws. Returning to the kitchen, he sat down next to his son and sighed, a sign that another tough day at the office had ended. Hearing the chair scrape across the linoleum, his wife turned around.

"Oh, hello," she murmured.

Harry sniffed in response and gazed into his whiskey glass. Denise shrugged and returned to her potatoes. Harry looked over at his son. Spencer's face was thrust between the pages of a comic. Leaning across the table, Harry removed the comic from the boy's grasp and dumped it on the chair next to him.

"Why do you let him read this stuff?" he said to his wife. "He's always got his nose in some rag … the least we can do is make sure he's reading something useful!"

There was no outward reaction from Spencer. He stared at his father, then climbed off his chair, picked up his comic and moved to go to his bedroom.

"Where are you going?" said Harry. We're eating now, right?"

"The potatoes aren't cooked yet," said Spencer, returning to the kitchen table. "Don't you have to cook the potatoes first?"

"These potatoes are not for us," replied his mother. This took a moment to sink in with Harry.

"What you mean, 'They're not for us,'" he said. "Who else do you cook for in this house?"

"It's for Mother. I'm going over there later."

"Can't she peel her own potatoes?"

"She can, yes, but her arthritis is playing up and she asked me if I could. It's just this one favor."

Harry closed his eyes, calculating whether it was worth the trouble starting a row when he was this tired. He took a deep breath.

"Well, how about doing us this one favor? How about cooking the pair of us a decent meal, on time and on this table when I get home? How about that, huh?"

He threw down his napkin and stormed out of the room, knowing that although he had started the argument, he did not have the gumption to finish it. Denise refused to be drawn in. Her only reaction was to grit her teeth and peel each potato with renewed vigor.

Spencer looked from his Mother over to his Father's empty chair, shrugged and continued to read his comic. Harry returned to the table without his jacket and tie but with another scotch. This time Denise looked up.

"I saw Mavis Williams in the supermarket today," she said. "Did you know that her Adam is working for the Tribute now? Apparently, they all received two months' salary as a Christmas bonus. Now that's a company I'd like to work for ... he gets six weeks off a year, a company car ... private health benefits ..."

Harry stopped her there. He took another swig from the tumbler and then slammed it on the table.

"I know exactly what they get at the Tribute, OK? In fact, I know exactly what they get in every metropolitan newspaper in England, thanks to you. Your knowledge of the working terms and conditions of the newspaper industry, in the year of our Lord, 1985, never ceases to amaze me. However, if you knew the working terms and conditions of the Great British Housewife, I would feel much happier."

Denise smiled to herself.

"Did you have a good day at the office, dear?"

"Yes, thank you, sweetness and light," replied Harry, with equal sarcasm. He noticed that Spencer was reading the comic again.

"I thought I told you to stop reading that rubbish!"

Spencer stood up, folded the comic under his arm and walked upstairs to his bedroom. He thought of slamming his bedroom door, but that would be too much.

Spencer's bedroom was his sanctuary. His mother rarely ventured in — except when laundry was a necessity — and he could not remember the last time his father had crossed the threshold. If by chance his Father had wandered in he would have noticed that — unlike many other 10-year old boys — Spencer's bedroom walls were not adorned with photos of exotic cars, football stars or hirsute rock 'n' rollers. Instead, hundreds of pages ripped from comic books hid the fading wallpaper. Spencer wished he were a better artist, but made up for it by being an imaginative writer. He had overwritten many of the speech bubbles with his own text, which — in his opinion — greatly improved the stories.

Spencer stared aimlessly at a small, portable black and white TV set. It was without a remote but that did not stop him changing channels, searching for something — anything — that was worth watching. Finding nothing, he returned to his latest comic. Using a blank sheet of paper, he cut out numerous speech bubble shapes and glued them over the original words in the comic book. Then he sat back, chewed the end of his pencil and waited for inspiration to take hold. *How would his Superheroes get out of this one?* he thought … and thought, and … nothing. Inspiration was on holiday, too.

Spencer clambered over his bed and gazed aimlessly out the window. The sky was low and the clouds reflected a dim, yellowish glow from the few street lamps that were still working. The wind tugged at the remaining leaves on the sickly beech tree behind the garden shed.

Wait … what was that in the shed? Spencer thought he saw a faint light, maybe from a glowing cigarette. He peered through the evening gloom. *There it was again!* This was puzzling … not even his dad would venture out on a night like this for a quick smoke in the shed. Anyway, he could hear his father's favorite TV quiz show blaring from the front room.

Spencer tucked his comic into his back pocket, padded down the stairs and grabbed the flashlight that hung from the umbrella stand. He pulled on his coat and boots, cracked open the back door and headed out into the night.

He made his way down the path that led to the shed, repeatedly shaking his flashlight in a vain attempt to get something more than just a weak, flickering beam. He stood on tiptoes and peered through the dirty windows, trying to find anything unusual among all the broken garden furniture, rusted machinery and abandoned projects that were strewn about inside. Unable to see anything clearly, he slipped the latch on the door.

Inside, the shed was dark and crammed with all sorts of odds and ends that made silent navigation impossible. Spencer shined his flashlight in a slow arc, its narrow beam picking out mementos from days past; his first skateboard; a deflated and mildewed plastic paddling pool; that old greatcoat that his dad wore… *Wait! His dad never had a coat like that. He was a 100 percent imitation Burberry man.*

Spencer moved in for a closer inspection when something caught his eye. He swung his flashlight over to identify the source. Spencer smelled the stale acridity of tobacco in the air. He held his breath and listened for any movement. The beam of his flashlight settled on a mass of crumpled newspapers in the far corner, where he heard a faint rustling. Spencer squinted through the gloom and picked out the rhythmic rise and fall of the newspapers along with the unmistakable rasp of a gentle, chesty ... snore. At that moment -- as he recognized the sound that rose from deep within the pile of newspapers — the beam of his flashlight settled on a section of the papers that had parted to reveal ... the bearded and wizened face of an old man.

Spencer staggered backwards in a hasty retreat, tripping over a rusty lawnmower. As he reached out to break his fall, the only thing within his grasp was a metal shelf, also the final resting place of a stack of half-empty paint cans.

It would have taken a great deal of purposeful effort for Spencer to have made any more noise as each can slid from the shelf and onto the concrete floor of the shed. Spencer winced as each can hit with a clang.

The old man sat straight up, confused and blinking. A grimy tea cosy sat atop a mass of tangled and tousled hair. A pair of battered, wire-rimmed glasses were perched delicately on a boxer's nose. His face was lined and weather-beaten from too many nights spent under the stars. His eyes, however, were sharp and clear.

"Who's there?" demanded the old man. "Who is it? I'm not afraid, I can handle myself. Come out where I can see you."

Spencer stayed in the shadows, rubbing a shoulder dinged by a falling paint can. The old man shielded his eyes.

"Well ... what do we have here?" said the man. "Come closer so I can take a good look at you."

Spencer did not move.

"Come on. You're not afraid of an old thing like me, are you?" Don't believe that stuff about me being able to handle myself. I've still got my glasses on and I never fight with my glasses on and I always wear my glasses, so that's OK, right? Come on over here."

Spencer shuffled forward so the man could see him better.

"Anyways, I haven't been in a real scrap since I was in the navy and that must have been, oh, let me see, before you were born, I'd say."

Spencer's curiosity was piqued.

"You were in the Navy?"

"Twenty years, man and boy. That's what give me these itchy

feet. Never can stay in one place for long."

"My father gets those," Spencer said.

"What's that?"

"Itchy feet. He says it's because of the nylon socks my mum buys him. He says all he needs is some quality cotton product and he can do without all that talcum powder."

The old man chuckled. "He's right, too! You can't beat nature's fabrics … and I should know more than most."

"Why is that?" asked Spencer.

"'Because I've spent more nights out alone under the stars than you've had hot dinners, I reckon. It's at those times that you get to appreciate them good fabrics what nature gave us."

"You sleep outside?"

"You bet, kid. Underneath the stars, gathered 'round a bonfire … a few friends, a nice cup of tea to keep body and soul together. Lovely, it is!

"Sounds like the Boy Scouts." Spencer said.

"Well, no, I'm not exactly a boy scout. I'm what you'd call a gentleman of the road, a vagabond, a bag man."

"You're a tramp?"

"Well, no offense taken, son," the old man said. "I suppose that's one way of putting it, although we prefer 'Gentlemen of the Road.' I've still got a little bit of pride left, you know."

Spencer was embarrassed. "Sorry, it just slipped out."

"I'm just messing, with you," said Nobby, looking around. "Besides, this place is hardly Buckingham Palace, is it? Who lives here?"

"I do," said Spencer, relieved that he had not offended his guest. "Actually, I don't live here, I live in our house. This is just where we store stuff when we don't need it."

The old man was incredulous.

"You're telling me you don't use this stuff, kid? That's an awful waste. There are things here that I could really use. As a friend of mine was saying just the other day, 'Nobby', he says, 'people don't use half the things they've got these days.' And you know what? I had to agree with him… 'cause it's true.

"Nobby? That's your name?"

"It's as good a name as any, ain't it? Maybe you'll never hear of a king or a ballet dancer called Nobby, but I can't see why that should bother me."

"Nobby, yes. I like it. Nice to meet you, Nobby. I'm Spencer." Spencer held out his hand in a fake formal greeting. Nobby stood up, brushed all the newspapers away and pumped the boy's hand.

"Nice to meet you, too, your highness. Now, where was I? Oh yes. You'd be amazed to know what you can do with everyday household objects. Take that watering can, for instance. Did you know that with only the smallest of adjustments you could transform it into a modern hydroelectric power generating system? A friend of mine says to me, 'Nobby,' he says, 'all it takes is a bit of applied skill, and you could create enough power to more than double what you use at the moment.' Now take that hosepipe …"

Nobby's monologue was interrupted by yelling from within the house.

"Well, if you don't like it, you know where the fridge is. Make your own dinner!"

Denise's voice reverberated down the garden path and into the shed. Spencer heard his mother stomp to the foot of the stairs and shout up to his room.

"You can come down now; your dinner is on the table." She waited for a response, but received none and marched back into the kitchen.

Back in the shed, Nobby was regaling Spencer with stories from the field.

"You really did that?" asked Spencer. "What did he say?"

"What could he say? He had never seen a scarecrow playing the penny whistle before, had he? He stood there with his mouth wide open until I finished. Then he climbed on his combine harvester and drove off to tell his missus, I suppose."

"Weren't you cold?"

"To be honest, in the winter it was brutal out there," Nobby continued. "Even natural fabrics won't keep body and soul together. That is why we come into the city, to find some artificial warmth. Even here —with all this technology around us — it's becoming a real problem to find warmth at night.

"You could sleep here," said Spencer.

"Thanks, kid," Nobby replied. "It's not just me, though. There's a whole bunch of us, and somehow, I can't see your mum and dad welcoming us into their garden shed, can you? Something about keeping house prices up in the area, so I'm told."

"Where do you sleep now?"

"Fleet Street."

Spencer's eyes widened. "No!" he said. "My dad works on Fleet Street! He works for The Scribe."

"Really? I don't think I know him. Mind you, we probably move in different circles. Does he sleep on the street, too?"

"No, of course not!" Spencer looked at Nobby to see if he was serious.

"It's not that bad. You see, while your dad is leaving work to go home in the evening, the newspaper presses are just starting up, preparing to print the next day's papers. When that happens, all these old printing machines create a lot of heat. That heat has to go somewhere and right now, it gets blown into vents and then out through grates onto the pavements around Fleet Street. That goes on all night long. So that's where we sleep. It's like having our own central heating system, only it's outside. Lovely! Snug as a bug in a rug, even on the coldest nights."

Spencer frowned. "So, what's the problem?"

"Technology," replied Nobby, suddenly serious. "New technology, see? What with everything getting more and more competitive and with them newspaper publishers seeing their profits dwindle, some of them have decided to 'rationalize.'"

Nobby motioned for Spencer to move closer and whispered, conspiratorially.

"We have it on very good authority that there are plans to move out of the city and set up somewhere cheaper in the sticks. And when one newspaper does that, then the rest will have to follow like a load of sheep. They're afraid that if one does something on their own, they might gain an advantage, so everyone follows along."

"Why don't you follow them too?"

"Oh, were it that easy, kid. Technology again, see? Technology and electronics and computers. It's all electronics and computers now, and there's no warmth in them. Coldest thing ever invented if you ask me." Nobby paused to consider this before he continued. "The newspapers are building their new headquarters out in cold, industrial wastelands. Built to their own specifications. They're worried about the competition, but they're also worried about their own workers. Unions and all that. These new premises will be built like Fort Knox. Barbed wire, concrete … the whole Alcatraz deal."

Nobby paused, and then broke into a grin as if sharing a private joke with himself.

"We're not beaten yet, though. We've got something planned for them. We're going to have warm beds and blankets for years to come if everything goes to plan."

Spencer was puzzled, but before he could ask another question, Nobby bounded out of the pile of newspapers and shooed him out the door.

"That reminds me, it's about time you got yourself up to bed. I'm used to it, but this is no place for a young buck like you to be spending his winter evenings. Now … hoppit!"

"But Nobby!" Spencer pleaded.

"Don't 'but Nobby' me. I know what's best for you."

"You'll be here in the morning?"

"Where else am I gonna go, eh?" And here, don't forget this." Nobby handed Spencer his comic that had slipped out of his pocket during his fall. "It looks great; what is it about?"

"Well," said Spencer. "These Superheroes are fighting against the forces of darkness…"

Nobby pointed at the blank speech bubbles.

"They look like they don't have a lot to say for themselves."

"The writing in these comics is not very good," Spencer said. "So, I replace it and write my own stories instead. I'll go get one that I've completed so you can read it."

"You know what? Show me tomorrow. You'll be fighting the forces of parental darkness if you don't hurry."

Nobby jostled Spencer with a couple of pretend jabs before closing the door and retreating into the shed.

"See you in the morning, then," Spencer said to the door. He reluctantly backed up the path, into his house and crept upstairs. He took one last look at the shed before climbing into bed. Outside, the wind had picked up again. It swirled between the side of the house and the garden shed, carrying with it an almost unworldly, whistling tone.

2. LAND OF OPPORTUNITY

The next morning Spencer was up early. Fully dressed, he bounded past his bleary-eyed mother as she opened her bedroom door to make the first cup of tea of the day.

"Hey," she called out as he leapt down the stairs. "Where were you last night? Your dinner was stone cold. Your dad had to finish it in the end."

"Wasn't hungry. See you soon. Eat later. Bye," Spencer, said, bounding out the back door and down the path to the shed. He gingerly opened the door, not wanting to startle the late sleeper.

"Nobby!" he hissed into the darkness. "Nobby ... it's me!" Not hearing a reply, Spencer ventured farther into the shed. "Nobby!"

Still nothing. Spencer frantically pawed through the discarded newspapers hoping to find the previous evening's raconteur. However, he soon realized that he was alone in the shed. Disconsolate and disheveled from rummaging among the papers, he sighed and gave up the search. The old man had gone.

Spencer stomped back up the path, slammed the back door and began to walk up the stairs. Then something crossed his mind. He stopped and walked back into the kitchen and sat down next to his father at the kitchen table.

"Dad, are all the newspapers moving away from Fleet Street?"

Harry paused, cereal spoon stuck in his mouth, mid-crunch. A trickle of milk slowly dripped back into the bowl. Original thought was always processed slowly in this family.

Spencer saw his father's brow had furrowed and winced as he

11

realized how strange his question must have sounded.

"I read it in a magazine the other day," he continued, trying to sound casual. "It said that some newspapers might be moving out of the city. And I know you work at one, so I thought I'd ask."

His dad resumed chewing, ruminating on whether an answer was worth the effort at this time in the morning. It was. After all, didn't the boy need to start paying attention to the realities of life?

"Well, you see, son, it's a number of things. First and foremost, it's to decrease costs, and therefore concomitantly to increase the marginal productivity. Then there's the need to improve the product, reduce the deadlines, add colour, that sort of thing. Mainly, though, it's the unions."

Spencer's mother rolled her eyes.

"Don't start on that again."

"What do you mean, 'Don't start that again?' Harry said. "Let me tell you, there are men down there who work in the press shop who have two jobs. Two jobs! One is a day job, down at the fish market or something, one that doesn't require any brainpower. In the evening, they come to work the overnight shift at the paper. And what do they do when they get there? They punch in on the clock and then they go home to bed. Can you believe it! Then in the morning, they get up, come to work and punch out again! Then they go to their day job. Imagine that! And we pay them ridiculous amounts of money to do it! Just to sleep!"

"Now you don't know that's true," said Denise, already familiar with the story.

"Of course, it's true. And worse, besides! I heard of one fella …"

"What do you do there?" Spencer bravely interrupted the flow.

"Excuse me?" Harry said, slightly miffed at being stopped mid-monologue.

"You know … what is your job at The Scribe?"

"Circulation. I work in the Circulation Department. Didn't you know that?" He took one final spoonful of his cereal, tucked his newspaper under one arm, his gabardine over the other and left for work.

"No," Spencer said to himself. "No, I didn't."

Spencer decided it was no use waiting for Nobby to return. He had checked the shed three times since breakfast and the old man was just not there. School was out for the holidays, the weather was unfriendly, and the shops were full of potential Christmas presents. He wrestled his heavy, woolen duffel coat on, followed by his boots. He was only two steps from the front door and …

"Don't forget you have to walk Moet & Chandon this morning!" Spencer's mother leaned out of the kitchen window. In a prior moment of madness, and blinded by the desire to save enough money for a mint copy of Amazing Stories #2, Spencer had agreed to walk his grandmother's bad-tempered Pomeranians for a tiny fee. Now, the devil was calling in her side of the bargain.

"OK. I'll go 'round after lunch. See you later!"

If he hurried, he could make it to a couple of the bigger toy stores and still have time to drag the evil twins across to the corner store. Once there, the ancient tobacconist would pretend to make a fuss of them, if only because his grandmother still owed him money 'on the slate,' whatever that was.

Spencer leaned into the wind as he strode towards the High Street. He thrust his hands into his coat pockets, his hood pulled down tight, impervious to the people around him … a man on a mission. He stepped around a woman pushing a shopping cart, a traffic warden writing a ticket and a mummified busker playing Jingle Bells on a penny whistle. Spencer paused in front of the holiday window display of a minor toy store to check on any new arrivals that he might add to his Christmas list. At an entrance to the Underground Tube station, Spencer leapt down the steps, three at a time. The junction above was heavy with holiday traffic and it was easier — and warmer — to take the Tube entrance, cross the intersection under all the wheezing exhausts and come up the stairs on the other side. He dodged around the subterranean commuters and almost tripped over the tip jar of another cocooned street musician, also playing Jingle Bells on a penny whistle.

"Sorry!" he said.

Spencer hurried onwards for a few seconds and then stopped in his tracks. He was no student of Christmas music but there was something about the phrasing of this version that was familiar. Where had he heard it recently?

Spencer spun around to see the cocooned musician remove his hat and wink at him while he finished the chorus on the whistle.

"Nobby!" Spencer could not keep his happiness in. He bobbed and jigged along to the music, for a moment forgetting that the old man had vanished without a trace only a few hours earlier. Eventually, the last chorus was over and despite receiving only meager applause, Nobby took the deepest of deep bows.

Spencer was still clapping enthusiastically until he remembered how Nobby had disappeared.

"Hey!" he said. "What happened to you?"

"What happened to me?" replied Nobby. "Ah, sorry, kid, I needed to run an errand."

Spencer frowned. "I thought I'd never see you again. Why didn't you leave me a note or something?"

Nobby paused for a second and then crouched down to Spencer's eye level.

A note, eh?" he said quietly. "Now how would that look if someone else came into the shed, hmm? And besides, I don't have a pen."

Nobby stood up, quickly counted all his tips and strode off across the underpass. "Now come on, Spencer, we've got work to do. This is prime time!"

Spencer hesitated for half a second before he followed Nobby up the steps and back into the winter wind. He had a hard time keeping up with the old man, who was surprisingly adept at avoiding the throngs of holiday shoppers.

"You see, kid, it's like this," said Nobby, deftly sidestepping a stroller. "Some people are born rich; some make it rich; some never find richness. Now if you think it's cash I'm talking about, you'd be wrong. Money doesn't make you rich. Well, it does, but that's not the kind of richness I'm talking about. No, I mean the richness of life. What you have seen and done in your life, not how big your Jacuzzi is or how many bonds you've got accumulating somewhere … know what I mean?"

"Of course!" Spencer lied.

"It's people what's important." continued the old man." Who you have met, what you have talked about, how many friends you have? Stuff like that. Get my drift?"

Spencer nodded in agreement, but his focus was on trying to keep up with Nobby.

"Things like that get forgotten in today's world, especially at times like Christmas and the other holidays. Look around at all these people."

Nobby stopped, suddenly. So suddenly that Spencer ploughed right into the old man's back.

"I mean, just look at 'em. All they care about is if they can grab the right model at the right price and in the right colour." Spencer gazed up at Nobby and then around at the shoppers.

"Now, I'm not saying that money ain't important," Nobby added. "It's a matter of perspective, that's all. Now me, I just need enough money for some smokes, somewhere warm to stay, some room for my friends and perhaps a glass or two of homebrew once in a while. That wouldn't suit everyone, I know. It wouldn't suit them big men who run the newspapers, I do know that. They couldn't survive without an expensive lunch here, a Rolls Royce there, a vacation over there. They would stop at nothing to make sure they get them, too! Even if it means putting us folks back on the streets and looking for some kind of warmth in the middle of winter. The funny thing is, they're so blind searching for the next fast score that they wouldn't miss something if it was taken from right in front of their noses."

They had arrived at another Tube station, and Nobby began to set up for the next concert. This time, Spencer was a willing participant. While Nobby played the squeezebox, Spencer danced around him, holding the old man's tea-cosy hat as a tip jar. Finally, as the last chorus was about to end, Nobby played a particularly winsome final few bars. Spencer stopped his collecting and became quiet, listening carefully to Nobby's performance. Once it was over, he put the hat down and applauded -- and encouraged the crowd to do likewise.

"Thank you, thank you very much!" enthused Nobby, happy to hear the clink of change dropping into his hat. He began to count the coins.

"Two plus four, plus … what's this… a flippin' washer? Still, not bad eh, my boy?" Nobby tossed a twenty pence piece over to Spencer. "Here, this is for you."

Spencer juggled and caught it after three attempts.

"And this," said Nobby, holding out the penny whistle. "Hold on to it for me for a while, would you? Learn the classics. Jingle Bells, obviously, White Christmas, that charity thingy."

"Wow, thanks," said Spencer. He delicately examined the whistle as if it were an ancient artifact.

"Right then, I'm off," said Nobby, pocketing the rest of the change. Spencer looked at him aghast.

"Wait!" he blurted. "Don't go! What are you doing?"

"I'm off to visit some friends."

"But … wait … can I … how?" Spencer stuttered and stumbled, unsure how to start or finish his sentence. Nobby looked over at the boy and broke into a crinkly smile.

"Hmm. You wouldn't want to come with me, would you?"

"Could I?" Spencer smiled nervously, afraid of what Nobby's reply might be.

"Let's think about this for a minute," said Nobby, rubbing his beard thoughtfully. "We'd probably have to mess you up a bit so you'd fit in."

Spencer furiously mussed up his hair.

"And those clothes look like they were just ironed."

The boy grabbed handfuls of his sweater in a vain attempt to crumple it up.

"And who polished your shoes?"

Now, Spencer was confused. He looked down at his scuffed Nikes and then back up to Nobby.

"Gotcha, didn't I? Come on then. Follow me closely and don't talk until I say so. Some of this crowd can be a little sensitive if you look at them wrong."

Nobby strode towards the Underground turnstile and held an exit gate open, waving Spencer through.

"Come on, we haven't got all day," he said while directing Spencer through a maze of tunnels and onto a platform.

After what seemed an eternity of changing trains, connecting walkways, elevators, and escalators, the pair emerged from the Tube system and into the watery, winter daylight of an unfamiliar landscape.

Half-finished construction projects stood tall next to pre-war, bombed-out warehouses. New asphalt lay next to cobblestones. The old man and the boy ventured further east, and as they did so, the re-developed was replaced by the unrestored. Scrap metal yards and empty lots -- strewn with hazard-filled rubble -- now dominated. The contrast between the busy, high-street throb of traffic and the nearly deserted streets of this industrial wasteland was palpable.

"Nobby," said Spencer, nervously looking behind him. "What is this place?"

"Ah! This is a magic land." Nobby replied, theatrically opening his eyes wide. "A land once lost that soon will be reborn. A land that will rise like a phoenix out of the ashes. A land that will be re-incarnated as the land of opportunity."

"What are you talking about?"

"OK, so it's the Docklands renovation scheme, but if you believe what people have been saying about "urban rejuvenation" you'd think it was the flippin' Garden of Eden!"

The pair crossed the cobbled street and skirted around the burnt-out husk of a car. Spencer looked nervously over his shoulder at the cinder blocks that had long since replaced the wheels. Nobby continued onwards to an open square of ground, bordered on three sides by a partly demolished building. In the middle, a few men tried to keep warm by feeding an oil drum fire with discarded planks of wood. Nobby slowed, then dropped on one knee so that he was face to face with Spencer.

"OK," said Nobby. "I need you to stay here for a moment while I go talk to the boys."

"Who are they?"

Nobby looked furtively over at the group gathered around the fire.

"Friends of mine — but sometimes they can be a bit leery of strangers," he whispered. He winked at Spencer and then walked towards the fire. Spencer could not hear what they were saying but after a while, it was clear there was some disagreement. Palms were raised, fingers wagged and heads were shaken. Eventually, Nobby beckoned to Spencer.

"OK, kid, I'd like you to meet some of my mates. This here is Red."

Nobby gestured in the direction of a fair-skinned, redheaded man who underneath all the layers was probably only in his early 20s. Red kept his hands in his pockets and thrust his jaw at Spencer in a grudging semblance of a welcome.

"This is Caractacus." Older than Red — but just as intimidating — Caractacus fixed Spencer with his one good eye and looked him up and down. A patch covered Caractacus' other eye and the patch itself had an eye crudely drawn on it. Spencer withdrew a little farther behind Nobby.

"And last, but not least, this is Kipper."

In front of him stood the wildest-looking individual Spencer had ever seen. Tall and thin, and covered in layers of dirty, disintegrating clothing, Kipper towered over the other men as he warmed himself by the makeshift brazier. His pressed his palms so close to the flames that the smoke curled up through the fingerless gloves. Wild, curly black hair covered most of his head. It tumbled out at all angles from underneath a filthy woolen hat, so that only his eyes were visible through the smoky haze. He looked Spencer up and down, slowly stroking his long, tangled beard as if he was trying to make a decision. Finally, he strode purposely at the boy and thrust out a filthy hand.

"How ya doin', wee man? Nice to meet a friend of Nobby's," he said.

Kipper's rough brogue rolled off his tongue and seemed to float towards Spencer like the tendrilled fingers of an animated aroma.

"Nobby's been telling us a lot about you." he continued. "Spencer is it? Nice to meet you, Spencer." Kipper grabbed Spencer's hand and pumped it vigorously. Spencer tried to withdraw but Kipper was having none of it.

"Ach, no need be afraid of me, son. I'm just an old softy. Isn't that right Nobby?"

"Soft as a baby's bottom, Kipper, to be sure," said Nobby, before leaning over and whispering out of the corner of his mouth. "And smells like one, too!"

"I know," Spencer quietly agreed. His eyes began to water as an otherworldly smell that emanated from deep within Kipper's rotting clothes enveloped him like a rancid blanket. It was definitely compost-y in nature, but there were was also hints of a meaty funk; a stale, rancidity and a touch of something recently deceased. Without a doubt, there were aspects of every unpleasant stench that Spencer had ever experienced. "What is that? It's terrible!" he said.

"What's that, wee man?" inquired Kipper, innocently.

"I was just telling him not to judge a book by its spots," Nobby said. "It could come up smelling of roses."

Kipper tried to process this. "I don't know about that," he said. "But I do know that if Nobby will vouch for you, that's good enough for me."

Spencer frowned. "Vouch for me?"

"Well, it's not good enough for me, and it won't be good enough for them, neither!" interjected Caractacus. "I mean, what do we know about this kid?"

Red hopped on the bandwagon. "Yeah, you never know what they might try next. Maybe he's a spy!"

Spencer anxiously looked at Nobby.

"Gentlemen, please!" said Nobby, putting a reassuring arm around Spencer. "Of course, he's not a spy."

"Oh yeah?" continued Caractacus. "What did you say his dad does?"

Nobby shook his head. "That's crazy talk. And as I told you before, young Spencer here can be a valuable resource."

"A resource?" said Spencer, his voice now quivering. "What do you mean, 'a resource'?"

"Nobby's right," said Kipper. "Come on, does this wee whippersnapper look like any kind of spy? Look at him; the poor wee thing is terrified."

All the men turned to face Spencer, who was sheltering behind Nobby. Caractacus and Red paused and then looked to each other. Finally, Caractacus shrugged.

"Ah, sorry kid. I guess we are a bit wound up, what with everything being so close, an' all."

"Yeah," agreed Red, sheepishly. "Sorry. No hard feelings, mate?"

"No. No hard feelings." Spencer tugged on Nobby's sleeve. "Nobby, what is this all about?"

"Sorry, kid. I know it's a lot to take in, but it will be worth it, believe me. Let's take you home, eh? But on the way, would you mind if we stopped off somewhere first? I want to show you something, something wonderful. I promise it's nothing bad and it will explain everything."

"I guess it's OK."

"That's the spirit!" Nobby tousled Spencer's hair before throwing a few fake punches that deliberately missed their mark.

"Come on, get your guard up. Watch out, here comes a right, now, a left hook. Jab, jab, jab!"

Spencer forgot his reticence as he danced around his new sparring partner, bobbing and weaving.

"Could you teach me to box?" Spencer asked Nobby.

"Hah! Sleep in a box, maybe," Red taunted.

"I could still box your ears," Nobby said.

"You'd have to catch me first, you old geezer!" Red laughed, as he and Caractacus headed back to the Tube station.

Nobby and Spencer followed, but made sure they were ahead of Kipper. No one wanted to be caught trailing in his wake.

The group entered the Tube station during the lunchtime rush. As the men descended the escalator, Spencer noticed that everyone appeared twitchy. Nobby confirmed this.

"Psst, Spence," he whispered. "Keep your eyes peeled, will you?" And if you see any blokes wearing a particular blue uniform, could you let us know?"

"The police?" Spencer said. "Are you in trouble?"

Caractacus laughed. "Ha! Not yet, son! But give us a minute and we'll see what we can come up with!"

They exited the escalator and walked along a tunnel, away from the main stream of passengers. The walkway twisted downward, and the men took several turns until Spencer was unsure if he would ever remember the way out. At this depth in the system, there were few passengers, even in rush hour. Finally, they came to an ancient door seemingly carved into the side of a corridor covered by a rusted metal gate, which Red pulled open. Kipper fumbled under his rotting clothing until he recovered a large key. He inserted it into the lock; the men put their shoulders to the door and pushed. It creaked and swung open.

"Quick. Get inside!" Nobby exhorted. He shepherded Spencer through the door, but not before the boy noticed a faded "DO NOT ENTER," sign screwed onto it. The door closed behind them and everything was suddenly pitch black.

"Hey, Red," Nobby said, "turn on that light."

Red flipped the switch, and an ancient light bulb flickered into life. Spencer turned to see where he was. It looked like some sort of maintenance room, full of old tools, wires, and other discarded equipment.

"A bit like your own shed, ain't it?" Nobby said to Spencer. "All right, Carrot," he continued. "You go first."

"My name ain't Carrot, as you flippin' well know," huffed Caractacus.

He turned to Spencer.

"Actually, Caractacus was a famous British General in ancient times. A great leader of men. And anyways, why do I always have to go first? I always bang my head on that beam."

"A general leads from the front," Nobby said. "Move it!"

"If I was a general I would flippin' do things differently, I can tell you," Caractacus said.

He sighed and shuffled off to the far end of the room. Once there, he shifted some pieces of dusty machinery to reveal an old ladder that descended through a hole in the floor.

"Ooh, me old bones," Caractacus groused as he descended the ladder into the hole.

"We're going down there?" Spencer asked.

"Of course," Nobby replied. "Is there a problem?"

"Uh, no. It's … it's fine."

"Me next!" said Kipper, moving swiftly towards the hole. "I can't wait!"

Suddenly, Nobby, Spencer, and Red all dashed for the ladder

"Kipper!" hissed Nobby. "You know you have to go last, so you can turn off the lights."

Nobby turned to Red and Spencer and gave them a secret thumbs up.

"Ach, it's not fair," remonstrated Kipper. He slouched away and flicked off the light switch, plunging everything into darkness again.

"Ow!" said Caractacus, as his head banged on a wooden beam.

"Not yet, Kipper. Not yet!" said Nobby. "OK, Spencer, off you go; just watch your head as you go down."

Spencer climbed down the ladder. He was a little underwhelmed when he reached another darkened room. It was full of pipes that ran along the ceiling, pushed out of the walls and sank down through the floor. The other three joined Spencer, and they clambered over the pipes, making their way to the end where another heavy steel door awaited them.

"OK, here we are," Red said. "No turning back now."

The word 'DAGNER' was stenciled in faded red ink on the door.

"What's Dagner?" Spencer enquired.

"Danger! It says Danger," Nobby said. "I was in a bit of a hurry then, and I am again now." He motioned to the other men.

"You boys go ahead. I want a quick word with Spencer before we go in."

Kipper nodded and flipped open the padlock that held the door closed. They pushed the door and it opened a few inches. Light flooded in from the other side. The men slipped through, closing the door behind them, leaving Nobby and Spencer alone in the dark.

Nobby lit a match and sat down on the floor. He pulled the remnants of a votive candle out of his coat and let the match heat the wax until it dripped onto the floor. Then he pushed the candle down onto the molten wax and lit the candle.

"Now, Spencer," he said. "You trust me, right?"

"Yes, of course." Spencer had forgotten his earlier reticence, his interest now piqued by what lay on the other side of the door.

"Good. So, I want you to promise me something,"

"Anything."

"No, not anything. Just this one thing. This and only this. I want you to promise me that you will never tell anyone outside of me and Red and Caractacus -- or any of the others that you will meet -- what goes on behind this door. Do you promise?"

Spencer was getting impatient. He really wanted to know what was behind that door.

"OK. I promise, I promise, I promise."

Nobby gently put his hand over the boy's mouth.

"Shh. That's enough with all the promises," Nobby said. "I never was too fond of them anyhow." He stood up and moved closer to the door.

"OK, here we go. Follow me closely and once you get inside, stay low. Ready?"

"Yes. Come on, let's go!" Spencer put his shoulder to the door and pushed but it would not budge. Nobby smiled and added his weight to the effort. The door opened and the pair slipped inside.

Back at his house, Spencer's mother was on the phone.

"Really? Yeah, he was supposed to go over this afternoon."

Denise used her shoulder to cradle the phone against her ear so that both hands could continue working on her fingernails.

"Chandon went all over your new rug? No, I didn't know it was a Qashqai. No, of course you don't pay him, Mum. I gotta go. Bye."

Denise hung up, sighed, grasped the nail file with both hands and pretended to plunge it into her chest.

"Oooh. That boy!"

3. THE CAVERN

Spencer found himself atop a balcony. His eyes slowly adjusted to the change in light, for the room below was brightly illuminated. Nobby tapped Spencer gently on the shoulder, then motioned for him to peek over the balcony. A cavernous hall, at least 30 feet tall from floor to ceiling, stretched out in front of him. On the floor, various men and women were engaged in all kinds of business. Some were on phones, others were writing or drawing at desks, many were walking quickly from one part of the room to another, carrying pieces of paper in the way that only extremely busy people did. At the far end of the cavern, a large, semi-circular train tunnel — dark and boarded up by a series of heavy planks — led to unknown blackness.

Spencer quickly took all this in, because most of his attention was focused on the object in the center of the hall. A massive machine — adorned with myriad cogs, rollers, pipes, wheels, stairs, railings, dials and levers — hissed and whistled as if it were a living, breathing entity. It almost reached the ceiling and was connected to a tangle of cables and hoses that gave the impression of a metal giant on life-support.

"Wow," Spencer said. "What is this place?

"Wonderful, ain't it?" Nobby said. "It's an old Underground station that was an early attempt to link the Tube lines under the river but they ran out of money and never finished it. This whole place had been bricked up for years before we found it." Nobby pointed to the dark tunnel. "See those tracks over there? They were never even connected to the grid."

"So, this is where you sleep?"

"Oh no, this place ain't ever had any maintenance, and the state of them tunnels ain't good at all. We're too deep and too close to the river for us to make this home."

Spencer gazed on in amazement. "So, what is everyone doing here?"

Nobby's eyes shone as he explained. "Remember I told you about all the newspapers leaving town for the suburbs and how that meant we might freeze in the winter?"

"Of course. I asked my father about it."

"You did, eh? Well, this is what we intend to do about it. This is our very own TV guide, our lifestyles section, our advice section, stars, gossip, news, finance, sports … the kit *and* the kaboodle"

"Don't forget the comics!"

"Some of the people down here have been living, breathing and sleeping with newspapers for most of their lives," Nobby said. "It's been in the tea leaves that the newspapers were moving away from Fleet Street, so for years we've been collecting stuff, piece by piece. And now we've decided to do something about it." He pointed to the machine that dominated the cavern.

"A little bit of machinery here, a little bit there. It's amazing how much you can pick up. Security in them press rooms was terrible, and there were so many times when the presses were idle, or times when the old presses were being replaced with new ones. All we did was to help ourselves to some of the surplus parts. Most of them hadn't been used in years and weren't missed. All that lovely machinery was just going to waste! We decided to do something with it, or at least Kipper did. The man is a genius with machinery. He could build a missile defense system out of Lego, he could."

As Nobby explained the plan, Spencer watched Kipper, his sleeves rolled up, welding something onto the machine. Men and women worked the phones; some stood next to a fax machine until the thermal paper had stopped spooling onto the floor. In a small office in the far corner, Red and Caractacus were talking to someone Spencer couldn't see through the grimy window.

"As you can see," Nobby continued. "We're building our own gravy train, our own money maker, our own printing press, our very own *newspaper*!"

"That's amazing!" Spencer said.

"These so-called press barons, all they think about is their circulations. We have to think of our circulations, too. Only our circulations are the ones that keep the blood pumping through our veins when it's 10-below outside."

"My dad talks about circulations too! He works in the circulations department."

"Is that right?" said Nobby, suddenly distracted. Meanwhile, the hum of conversation in the cavern had died down. Even Kipper had flipped up his welding mask. Everyone was staring up at the balcony.

"Spencer," whispered Nobby. "Come on, son. Gently does it." Nobby took the boy's hand and they stood up from behind the railing, making them fully visible to everyone below. A telephone rang. The man nearest to it picked up the receiver and — without bothering to find out who was calling — hung up, and returned his gaze to the pair at the top of the stairs. For a moment, there was silence before the office door opened, and a small, balding man stormed out and marched to the middle of the floor. He lifted a trembling and accusatory finger and pointed it straight at Spencer.

"Who is THAT?" His voice quivered with rage. "Grab him!" The words echoed around the chamber and the silent spell was broken. An angry mob quickly formed and swarmed towards the bottom of the stairs.

Nobby tried to calm them down. "Wait, wait, it's OK. The boy is with me!"

It was no use. The mob rose up the stairs, grabbed Spencer from Nobby's grasp and carried him away. Nobby, also manhandled by the mob, fought to stay with the boy.

"Help, help!" cried Spencer. He struggled to free himself from the mob but they had lifted him above their heads and carried him away. Nobby likewise struggled to get free. He saw the panic in the boy's eyes.

At that moment, Kipper vaulted down from his machine and battled his way across the room. He grasped the small man by the collar and whispered frantically into his ear. At first, the man fought to free himself, but as Kipper continued, he calmed down and listened. Then he turned to the throng.

"Enough!" he yelled. "Put them down!" They lowered Spencer to the ground and released Nobby. The small man pointed to each of them.

"You. And you. In my room, now!" Nobby looked over at Spencer and gave him a nervous thumbs-up. The pair were ushered into the office and the door closed behind them. The small man made his way over to his chair, sat down and put his feet up on his desk. As he did so, Spencer silently mouthed Nobby a question. Nobby did not see it but Kipper did and quietly whispered in the boy's ear.

"That's the Editor. He's the one who is going to make this all happen." Spencer recoiled at being so close to Kipper, but nodded anyway.

"So," began the Editor, fixing Spencer with a beady eye. "How do you like this place?"

Spencer moved behind Nobby, so that there was someone between him and this grimy little man who was interrogating him.

"You, boy. I'm talking to you."

"It's, uh, brilliant!" Spencer replied nervously.

"Brilliant, eh? Yes, it is, isn't it? All quite brilliant." The Editor hooked his thumbs into the pockets of his equally grimy waistcoat and learned back is his chair.

"And do you know what else is brilliant, young man? What else is brilliant is that we are on the edge… the cusp, the precipice, of greatness here."

"That's, uh, nice," Spencer said. The Editor looked at Spencer aghast.

"Nice?" he said. "Nice? No, this is not nice! This is not a nice business at all! And I should know. I've spent the last 30 years around this business. Every single day, the delivery trucks pulling up before daybreak to get their papers loaded have woken me. I've been woken by the hacks — also loaded — falling out of the bars at midnight. I've been woken by the presses starting up in the middle of the night just as I was dozing off."

"Sounds like you need to find a better place to lay your head, Guv'nor." joked Caractacus who had sneaked into the office with Red.

The Editor closed his eyes, signed heavily and continued.

"Nice? No this is not a nice business. The newspaper business is a foul, dirty thing. And you know what? That's what people want. So, let's give them want they want. They want dirt. They want muck.

They want filth. And let's face it, son ....""

The Editor stood up and leaned across his desk until his face was only six inches away from Spencer.

"...Who knows more about dirt and muck and filth than us?"

Spencer backed away until he was stopped by the rear wall of the office.

"Hey, hey," interrupted Nobby. "You're scaring him."

"Really?" the Editor said. "I'm scaring him, am I? Well, sometimes it's good to be scared. It's good to know how serious we are, how secret this place is. You understand that, right?"

Spencer nodded vigorously, hoping that that the interrogation was over.

"Excellent!" The Editor's demeanor was suddenly brighter. "Kipper, give the young man the tour, please. Nobby, could I have a word?"

Kipper shepherded Spencer out of the office. "Don't worry yerself, son." Kipper nodded towards the Editor. "His bark is way worse than his bite. Now, let me show you around ma kingdom. Stay close, though."

Spencer was conflicted. He did not want to get too close to Kipper because of the smell, but he did not want to stray too far from him, either, in this strange, unfriendly cavern. He chose the familiar funk over the wary, untrusting eyes of the men and women whose day this child had interrupted.

Kipper cleared his throat. "Relax everybody," he said loudly. "This wee man is Spencer. He's OK. You're going to be seeing more of him from now on. Let's make him welcome, eh?"

Kipper took a firm grip of Spencer's arm and led him over to a pair of men huddled around a desk.

"These gentlemen are some of our journalists." He nodded in their direction. "Jacko, Suds, I'd like you to meet Spencer."

"Our pleasure, I'm sure," leered Suds as he scanned Spencer from head to toe.

Spencer nervously held out a hand for Suds to shake but the old man just looked at it as if it was a fish, not a forearm.

Eventually, Spencer looked down at it also, wondering why he had offered it in the first place. He was just about to withdraw it when — from out of nowhere — a gnarled and wizened hand suddenly grabbed his wrist from behind.

"Hey kid!" rasped a broken-edged voice. "Can you lend an old geezer a bob or two for a cuppa?

Spencer desperately tried to pull away, but the grip on his arm was too strong.

"Come on. I know you're hiding some cash somewhere on you. Where is it?" The old man attempted to put his hand in Spencer's pocket, but Kipper was having none of it.

"Away with you, Bangers! Leave the boy alone," Kipper said, pulling the old man's hand from Spencer's wrist and ushering him past the desks.

"Who was that?" Spencer hissed through closed teeth.

"Ah, that was Bangers, our financial correspondent. Stay clear of him," Kipper said, continuing the tour. "Here is our entertainment section, crosswords, horoscopes and the like." He motioned towards a man hunched over his desk, scribbling something on a dirty scrap of paper.

"This here is Shoulders."

Shoulders looked up and peered at Spencer through massive, coke-bottle glasses that made his eyes look huge.

"Here's looking at you, kid," he said before returning to his scrawl.

"Shoulders is our film critic," Kipper said proudly. He's seen probably dozens of films, so I'm told."

"That's right," Shoulders said. "Wanna see one with me?"

"What's it called?" Spencer asked.

"'Death in Bermondsey.' It's an intercultural rom-com set on a council estate. One's a Bengali rapper, the other is a…" Shoulders paused and peered at his scrap of paper.

"Dammit. I can't read my own writing. Anyway, they both die in the end. You two wanna go?"

"There's not much point now, is there?" said Kipper. "Now that you've told us the plot."

"Thanks, but I think I'll pass this time," Spencer said. The pair moved on to the next desk, leaving Shoulders to re-writie his scribble.

"And here is our new diarist, our gossip columnist," Kipper said with a flourish. "Ta-Da!"

Spencer had been so preoccupied with meeting all these strange new people that he had not seen Nobby leave the Editor's office.

Now he was face to face with him across a desk.

"Nobby... It's you?" he said.

"And why not, may I ask?" replied Nobby, proudly pulling an old-time reporter's green visor down over his mass of thatched hair. "Anyway, I'm not merely a purveyor of tittle tattle. I'm the new court and social reporter."

"What happened to the old one?" Spencer said.

"Last week he crashed a big society ball," Kipper said. "He became way too social and got caught!"

Kipper laughed loudly at his own joke. Spencer smiled politely, expecting to share the humor with Nobby. However, Nobby was distracted. The door on the balcony had opened. A woman had quietly entered and was now peering through the gloom. Her greying hair was teased and unkempt, her eyebrows were painted and her bright red lipstick was slightly smeared over a heavily rouged, careworn complexion. Eventually, she saw Nobby. She waived and began to descend the stairs. Nobby rushed over and offered her a hand, which she took daintily and somewhat regally.

"You look gorgeous, as always," remarked Nobby, his eyes shining in admiration.

Spencer could not help but notice that the woman's clothes seemed mainly to consist of torn plastic bin liners held together by a complex assemblage of fabric, bull clips and other bits and pieces.

"Oh, thank you, dear," she replied. "It's so gratifying when someone acknowledges when you've made an effort."

Kipper learned over and whispered to Spencer. "That's Mavis. She's the ..."

"Fashion editor?" Spencer ventured.

"That's right. You're getting the hang of it now." Kipper leaned over and whispered in Spencer's ear. "Aye, and she's also Nobby's girlfriend," Spencer looked up at Kipper in wonderment.

"Spencer, I'd like to introduce you to a friend of mine," Nobby said. This vision before you is Mavis." Spencer smiled nervously.

"Charmed, to be sure," Mavis said.

"How do you do?" Spencer said.

"Fabulous! I've had such a day! Hemlines are down again. You don't know what a blessing that is for people who have to work on a limited budget. My hems, for instance are always coming down. And the colours! Oh, those colours. Winter is the cruelest month for colours, my dear." Nobby gently interrupted.

"Now, dear," he said. "I'm sure that the boy has more important things to think of than colours and seasons. Isn't that right Spencer? Besides, I'd like a quick word with him, if I may. I think I owe him an explanation."

"Nae so fast, Nobby!" said Kipper pulling Spencer close. "The boy has met everyone except the most important person of all. Come on, Spencer, you have to meet ma wee baby."

Kipper guided Spencer to the huge piece of machinery that dominated the cavern.

"Five years. Five long years this has taken me. The strife I've had with it! Every nut, every bracket; each single small screw we had to free from the other presses. So many nights I spent sneaking into the guts of the machinery at the other newspapers … waiting. Waiting for the night watchman to fall asleep so I could start work. Loosen a bolt here; turn a screwdriver there; remove a pair of lithographic offset plates over there. And at any moment I could have been discovered — or worse! They weren't using the presses for anything, they were just sitting there, dead. And now, now I've brought them alive."

Kipper's voice had become progressively louder until everyone in the cavern had stopped what they were doing.

"Ahem. Kipper, it's still a printing press, right?" Nobby said quietly to his friend.

"Ah Nobby," Kipper sighed. "Was Tin Man just a piece of tin? Was Herbie the Love Bug just a wee bug?"

"Well actually, they were imaginary," Spencer suggested.

Kipper refused to be sidetracked. "No, this is a living, breathing thing!"

"Not yet, it's not," Nobby said. "You've never started the thing up."

"Details, details," Kipper said impatiently. "Don't worry yourselves, we're powering her up tonight. She'll live. You'll see. You'll all see!"

Kipper climbed on top of the machine, pulled a screwdriver out from under his rags and began tightening a few screws here and there.

"Carrot, hand me that oil can, will you?"

Caractacus climbed up on the press and handed Kipper the can.

"It ain't Carrot!" he said.

"Sorry, General, that's right." Kipper winked at Spencer. "Just having a wee bit of fun."

"At my flippin' expense, as usual." moaned Caractacus. "'Hey, what does this do?" He fiddled with a large lever on the machine but before the gears could engage, Kipper vaulted in front of him and yanked his hands from the controls. Kipper's eyes blazed.

"Never touch that. Do you understand?"

"I was just having a bit of a joke," Caractacus said.

"Never!" He shooed Caractacus away.

"Blimey," Caractacus grumbled. "Sensitive geezer, ain't you?"

Nobby gently elbowed Spencer and nodded towards the exit. Then he blew Mavis a kiss. She motioned that she had some writing to take care of. No one wanted to distract Kipper, so Nobby and Spencer tiptoed up the stairs and swung open the metal door.

"Hey, kid!" yelled the Editor from outside his office. "Remember. You have seen or heard nothing of this place!" Do you understand?"

"I think so sir. Yes sir." Nobby put an arm around Spencer's shoulders and quickly ushered him out the door.

***

Across town, in the print room of another major metropolitan newspaper, a technician frowned at his clipboard. He ran his finger slowly down the checklist and then looked over to where faded carpet tiles outlined the shadow of a missing piece of machinery. He could not expect to find every small piece from the inventory list that was his assignment, but he found almost nothing of what was supposed to be right in front of him.

"Really?" he sighed. "Could anyone have bothered to tell me that the typesetter had been shipped already?"

***

Spencer and Nobby navigated their way through the Tube system and found their way back to the surface just as the evening rush hour began. Nobby talked a mile a minute but Spencer was subdued.

"Do you see what we want to do, son?" said Nobby, his eyes

opening wide. "Do you see how it could all work? All we want to do is find somewhere quiet to retire to, just like regular folk. There's not so much wrong with that, is there? I know the boys didn't take to you so quick, but they'll come 'round. They've spent years putting all that together and they're nervous, that's all."

"Nobby," said Spencer. "Back there in the cavern. What did you mean when you said I could be of use to you?"

"Oh, that." Nobby shifted uneasily.

"Yes. That."

"Sorry about that. It just came out wrong. I didn't mean it to sound so harsh." He took Spencer's hand and guided him over to a park bench.

"OK, this ain't easy. What I meant was that you can be of use to us, but that doesn't mean that we are going to use you. Do you understand?"

"No." Spencer replied curtly.

"Perhaps I haven't explained myself very well. Remember when you told me that your dad was in newspapers?"

"Yeah," Spencer replied cautiously.

"Look at all the people you met in the cavern. Journalists, advertising staff, production, and all that. Well, what is missing?

Spencer shrugged. "I don't know."

"Distribution! It's distribution, see! We know nothing about that. We know production because we have the machinery and Kipper is a mechanical wizard. We know the news because we've been reading it, sleeping with it — sometimes eaten it."

"You've eaten newspapers?"

"Sure, when times were tough. My advice, though, steer clear of the advice columns. Indigestible, if you ask me. Now advertising! We all know about advertising. Let me tell you, if you searched the gutters around Fleet Street at about 4 in the afternoon on any weekday, you would find more media directors and account executives than you would the homeless. How often have I woken up next to an advertising hotshot who never recovered from his expense account lunch? We have so many contacts that we are confident in selling a bunch of ads. However, what we don't know is distribution. We know nothing about what happens to the paper once it leaves the plant."

"Nor do I," Spencer said.

"But you know someone who does."

"Oh no," said Spencer, shaking his head. "I can't ask him. We can't trust him."

"But he's yer Dad. He's family."

Spencer sighed. "I think I'm just in his way most of the time. I'm not sure he even really likes me."

Nobby laid a gentle arm around the boy's shoulder.

"No. I can't believe that. Why don't you try and talk to him?"

"I've tried that. I told him that I thought I'd make a pretty good comic book writer one day and he just snorted and said that sort of writing wasn't a proper job."

"Well, don't ask him outright. Be subtle. Most people like to talk about their jobs. Just prod him a little and see what he says."

"I know what he'll say! It's what he always says. He'll go on and on about the unions and then upper management and how new technology will put everyone out of a job."

"See." said Nobby. "He agrees with us already! Just try and find out the best way to get the paper into the hands of the everyday geezer."

Spencer ruminated for a moment. "Is there any other way? Because if there's no other way then I'll try and give it a shot."

"We can't think of another," said Nobby, rubbing his beard.

Spencer pursed his lips and nodded, solemnly.

"OK, then. I guess."

"That would be great. And one more thing. I was wondering if you could see yourself helping me out?"

"I already said yes," Spencer said.

"I know you did. I was thinking of something more particular. Something between you and me."

"What is it?"

Nobby took a deep breath. "OK. Here we go. Have you ever met a journalist who couldn't read or write?

"No, of course not."

"You have now."

Spencer frowned. Then the light bulb went on.

"Oh, Nobby!"

"I never learned, see? I can't tell the others that. They would never let me work on the paper, and I want this so much. Will you help me write the column? I can tell you are a good student, and it wouldn't be that much work. I'll dictate it and you can write it all down. How hard could it be?"

Spencer stood up and offered Nobby his hand.

"It would be an honor," Spencer said.

"Come 'ere!" Nobby said. He grabbed Spencer's arm and pulled him in for some mock wrestling.

"OK! Let's get you home, and we can start tomorrow. This is going to be so much fun, ain't it?"

The next morning, Spencer waited in his bedroom until he heard that everyone was downstairs eating breakfast. He took a quick peek out of his window before joining his family in the kitchen. Spencer's grandmother had joined his mum and dad.

"This is delicious, Denise," Spencer's grandmother said after demolishing a plate of bacon and eggs. She wiped the last smear of yolk with a thick slice of white bread and turned her attention to Harry.

"Thirty-two years!" she said, wagging a finger.

"Was it that long, Mum?" said Denise, placing a cup of tea onto the table.

"Thirty-two minutes, more like," whispered Harry to himself.

"I haven't had a drop for thirty-two years!"

"There was always a bottle of sherry open when I was over," said Harry.

"That was for visitors only."

"Such as your husband?" Harry whispered under his breath. A swift backhander from his wife was a forceful reminder that Harry needed to practice his whispering.

"Quiet!" hissed Denise.

"Hmm? What was that?" said Spencer's grandmother, looking up to see if she had missed something. Her gaze fell on Spencer.

"And you, young man. What happened to you yesterday? Moet & Chandon were beside themselves. They went wee wee all over the parlor, and that's the nicest room in the house."

"Yes," Denise said. "Where were you yesterday? Who were you with? Your dinner went stone cold. Your dad had to eat it in the end."

"That's right," Harry said. "Actually, it was better cold."

"The Vicar thought so, too," said Spencer's grandmother. "He was a teetotaler, you know? Thirty-two years without a lick of booze crossing my lips."

"Probably inhaled the gin vapor through the iron … Ow!" Harry rubbed the back of his head as another blow rained down.

"What time did you get in?" Denise asked Spencer.

"Not late. I wasn't hungry."

"Is this the last of the jam?" Harry asked.

"If you were out with those O'Reilly twins again, someone's going to get it!" Denise said, waiving a butter knife in her son's direction.

"It better not be. I only bought that jar last week," said Harry, taking the knife out of his wife's hand and scraping for the last of the jam.

"It was a shame he had to leave after that incident in the vestry, though," said Spencer's grandmother, licking her fingers one by one. Spencer walked over to the pantry, retrieved a full jar of jam and handed it to his father.

"Dad, how do you circulate a newspaper?"

"Those two are nothing but trouble. Their father was the same. Mark my words," said Denise.

"Good-looking though, for a man of the cloth," said Spencer's grandmother.

"Well, it's getting tough. All these free newspapers that are being given away are eroding our traditional markets," Harry said.

"They give the newspapers away?" Spencer asked.

"I wish your father could have given you away, Denise," sniffed Spencer's grandmother.

"Not now, Mum," sighed Denise.

"How do they make any money?" Spencer said.

"Why all the questions?"

"School project."

"They sell a lot of advertising and they have fewer staff." Harry looked at his watch. "Urgh! Coffee is cold. Gracious! Look at the time. Gotta run. See you later."

"Can I walk with you to the station?" Spencer asked. Harry paused for a second. This was unusual.

"OK. Let's go, then. Chop, chop."

Spencer jumped up from the table and followed his father out the door.

"School project?" said Spencer's mother, frowning. "What

school project? They've broken up for the holidays."

"People often break up over the holidays," said Spencer's grandmother. "The holidays put a lot of stress on a family. That's a fact."

"Not now, Mum," sighed Denise.

Having peppered his father with questions on his way to work, Spencer returned to his house and tiptoed down the side path. He made his way across the paving stones and quietly tapped on the door of the shed.

"Psst! It's me," he said. The shed door swung open and Spencer entered, pulling the door closed behind him.

4. PROPRIETARY INSTINCTS

Harry paced down the corridor and waited nervously for the lift. Arriving at The Scribe, he had not even enough time to make himself some more toast before the phone rang and he was summoned to the 13th floor.

"What on earth could be going on?" he mused.

Harry tried to think what he could have done to deserve this. He had never even been to the 12th floor and now he had to go to the *13th?* Perspiration dotted his forehead, as he repeatedly pressed the lift call button. His anxiety was somewhat relieved when Chalmers from Marketing scooted around the corner and then tried to play it cool. Obviously, he had been summoned also.

"Any idea was this is about? Chalmers asked, trying to be nonchalant.

"Not a clue," replied Harry, hoping that Chalmers had not seen him punching the call button.

"Bonuses, probably." Chalmers straightened his tie. They both smiled, nervously. As if! The bell rang and the lift doors opened. Inside, McKenzie — still wearing his fraying gabardine — barely noticed the new passengers. He pawed through the Machine Service & Maintenance Form A303B-Pt2 on his clipboard, hoping against hope that the missing items would miraculously appear and he could check them off as all present and correct.

"Where to, gents?" inquired the lift attendant as Harry and Chalmers stepped aboard.

"Thirteen, please."

"Ooh, you too, eh?" The attendant eyed the three of them before dramatically withdrawing a key chain from his waistcoat pocket. He inserted the key into the special hole marked, '13th floor.'

"Must be something important,' continued the attendant, fishing for a clue.

"I sincerely hope not," murmured Harry.

The doors to the lift opened and the three men stepped out into a large, L-shaped anteroom. To their right, a pair of imposing wrought iron doors dominated the space like the entrance to a throne room. In front of them, set back against the far wall, was a small desk. It had a telephone and an intercom on it but nothing else. Behind it sat a young woman. She filed her nails and chewed gum at the same time. The three men nervously approached her.

"Excuse me," said Harry. The woman looked up and used her nail file to point them in the direction they were to follow.

"Thanks." Harry peeked around the corner of the room and let out a sigh of relief — at least it was not just him and Chalmers.

Before him, perched on a number of uncomfortable-looking chairs, were eight other department heads. Editorial, advertising, production, personnel, maintenance — a new man Harry could not place — and accounting, all looking equally concerned.

Harry nudged Chalmers in the direction of the stranger.

"Who's the new guy?"

"Mitchell. New security heavy," replied Chalmers, out of the corner of his mouth.

"Where's Legal?" whispered Harry.

"Shhh!" came the reply in unison. Harry, Chalmers and McKenzie sat down and waited. After a moment, Harry realized why it was so quiet. Everyone was straining to hear what was going on behind the double doors. They only had a second or two to wait before a voice boomed from inside the throne room.

"Definition One. '…being able to accept or tolerate delays, problems, or suffering… without becoming annoyed or anxious.' Definition Two! '…a person receiving or about to receive medical treatment.' Both are dictionary definitions of the word 'patient.' Be assured, Mr. Johnson, that if I were to lose the former, then you would swiftly join the ranks of the latter. May I remind you; I do not pay you for your opinions or for your hunches, I pay you only for what is and what is not admissible in a court of law. Do you understand? Do I make myself clear?"

Any response from the object of this fury could not be picked up by those outside the room, though all leaned forward, craning their necks to hear more of what might be happening inside. A loud buzzing broke the silence and the secretary pushed the button on the intercom.

"Yes, sir?"

"Herd the rabble in now, would you, please?"

The secretary turned to the department heads. "You may go in now," She pushed a button under her desk causing the iron doors to swing open. A small, sweaty man limped out and scampered through the doors marked "Emergency Exit."

"Legal." Chalmers nodded to Harry in the direction of the exiting minion.

The department heads stood up nervously. There was much checking of watches, straightening of ties, coughing and wiping of brows. Everyone was immediately busy and yet no one moved towards the door. The secretary looked up and sighed.

"Come on, you herd... you heard!" She bent down and grabbed an electric cattle prod. She pressed a button and it hummed, quietly.

"These are the times that make it all worthwhile," she said.

The secretary walked over to the executives and waved the prod over her head. Harry — being at the rear of the crowd — could not see what happened next, but he thought he heard a spark, a whimper and maybe the faint smell of barbeque. Anyway, the executives dashed through the door, all suddenly men of action.

Inside, the room was dark and quiet. The only noise was the shuffling of expensive shoes and the gentle hum of the cattle prod. Once everyone had squeezed in, the doors creaked shut. Out of the blackness came a voice — calm, this time — but still insistent.

"Two words, gentlemen. Who will be able to tell me which two words I have in mind? Both have twelve letters. Both begin with a vowel and end in a consonant. I am faced with the first while you are faced with the second. No clue so far? No takers, eh? No, I suppose not. I'm afraid I'm asking far too much of you. Let me put you out of your misery. The first word I have in mind is 'incompetency'. 'Unemployment' is the second. Do I make myself clear? Am I understood? Do I have to spell it out?"

Suddenly, the room filled with the light of a thousand spotlights.

The executives cringed as they tried to make out the figure standing in front of them. His knuckles rested on his desk as he leaned forward. A man of slightly less than average height stood in front of them. His three-piece suit strained as his barrel chest heaved; his eyes were wild and red-rimmed and his veined nostrils flared with every hyperventilated breath. His beard was specked with spittle, and his fist made a resounding thump as he bought it down sharply onto his desk.

"WHERE IS MY PRINTING PRESS?" screamed the Proprietor.

***

By its nature, Fleet Street held very few secrets. Soon enough, word leaked out that a whole printing press had been 'misplaced.' However, any semblance of schadenfreude among the other newspapers was tempered when reports began to surface that all was not right in their own kingdoms. A fax machine here, a typesetting machine there. As they began to take stock, it became clear that many newspapers had been somewhat careless with their inventory. At the Tribute, there was even a rumor that a whole week's supply of newsprint had just simply and quietly vanished.

***

The steel door creaked open, and Nobby and Spencer slid into the cavern. Inside, everyone was busy being busy. The journalists huddled together, the ad men worked the phones and the Editor watched everything from his corner office.

Kipper — perched atop his printing press — noticed Nobby and Spencer enter.

"Hey, wee man. Come and take a look at this." He beckoned at Spencer from atop the enormous contraption.

"Yes, good idea," said Nobby, directing Spencer towards Kipper. "I'll be over in a minute; I just have to talk to our friend over there." He walked over to the office, but stopped halfway and looked back at Spencer. "You said, 'Free,' right?"

Spencer nodded and began to climb the steps up the side of the printing press. Kipper beamed at him from the top step.

"Have you ever seen such beautiful gearing?" he said, as he

inserted a gleaming cog into position.

On the far side of the Cavern, Nobby grabbed the Editor and whispered in his ear. The Editor nodded, then pulled away to look at him in amazement as Nobby laid out his plan.

The Editor pursed his lips, tapped his foot and scratched his thinning dome. Thinking, thinking… then a decision.

"Hey, kid!" he yelled. Spencer looked up from Kipper's detailed description of more mechanical wizardry.

"Yes, sir?"

"I am reliably informed that you are in custody of information that is pertinent to the successful accomplishment of our desired aims."

"Huh?" Spencer shrugged. The Editor sighed.

"You know stuff, kid!" he yelled.

Mavis — who had been pouring over some fashion photographs on her desk — ran to Spencer's defense.

"Behave yourself, will you? Frightening the boy like that. And all he's trying to do is help us!" She laid a protective hand on Spencer's head.

"Anyway," she whispered to Spencer, "It seems from what they were discussing, that you have the best plan."

Spencer turned to face Mavis, away from Nobby and the Editor.

"How do you know what they were talking about?" he asked her.

Mavis winked at him. "Let's just say that there is an unintended benefit of having deafness in your family."

"You read lips?" mouthed Spencer, silently.

"When I have to," Mavis replied. "Our secret."

The Editor closed his eyes, drew a calming breath and walked over. "Yes, indeed, I am sorry. Please come into my office where we can discuss this, man to boy."

He stood aside and theatrically waved Spencer in.

Mavis, Nobby, Spencer and the Editor filed in, closing the door behind them. Kipper looked up from within his machine but all he could make out was a rather animated discussion.

Suddenly, the door to the cavern opened and Caractacus bounded through. He ran down the stairs and pushed his way into the Editor's office.

"Boss!" he wheezed. "They know!"

"They know what? Who knows what?" asked the Editor.

"All the regular newspapers and stuff," Caractacus said. "Our man on the inside said that they found out that some of their machinery and whatnot is missing. It's all that anyone was talking about."

"We've got to tell Kipper," Nobby said. "We'll have to bring the deadline forward."

"OK," said the Editor. "Calm down. We all knew that this was going to happen. There was no way to hide this level of larceny for such an extended amount of time." He opened the office door and bellowed across the cavern.

"Kipper! You nearly ready?"

"Aye, Boss. I just need to make a couple of wee tweaks here and there and we'll be all set."

"Good! Because we're bringing the publication date forward just as soon as we get the …"

The Editor stopped and tilted his head. Like everyone else, he had felt a faint rumbling coming from the abandoned train tunnel at the far end of the cavern.

"…newsprint."

The rumbling became louder. As Spencer peered into the darkness, he thought he saw a headlight, a flashlight, or some other kind of light coming from deep within the tunnel. Yes, there it was, then another and another. The beams grew stronger and the rumbling became louder as something big approached the entrance to the cavern. Spencer moved closer to Nobby and grabbed a handful of his greatcoat. There was something unsettling about the darkness and the vibration of whatever it was that was coming their way.

"Quick!" the Editor yelled. "Remove those planks." A group of men rushed over to the entrance to the tunnel and began removing the large planks that had blocked off the entrance.

"Nobby, go throw the switch."

Nobby walked a few feet into the tunnel and stood over the rail tracks that curved off into the darkness. As the tracks approached the entrance to the cavern, they split. One set finished at a brick wall while the other set branched towards the cavern. Nobby grabbed a large and rusty lever and with great effort, tried to move it. The switch refused to budge until he loosened it with a swift kick from the heel of his boot.

"Just needed a little persuasion, that's all," he said.

With a reluctant squeal, the lever moved. Nobby heaved at it again and the switch at his feet shifted the tracks so that they terminated at the cavern entrance.

Spencer peered into the darkness. In the distance, he made out a group of men approaching the cavern. Lights shone from helmets as the men pushed a rail cart along the tracks. Strapped to the cart was what looked to Spencer to be the World's Biggest Toilet Roll. A cylinder of paper more than six feet tall, held in place with numerous ropes and buckles, emerged from the darkness. Eventually, the men reached the edge of the cavern.

"Come on boys, give us a hand," said one of the men from as he removed his helmet and wiped his brow. "This thing is flippin' heavy!"

Although the man's face was dirty and covered in sweat, Spencer recognized Red, one of the men he had met around the fire in the Docklands.

The men cautiously maneuvered the massive cylinder of paper off the rail cart and onto the floor of the cavern and rolled it until it was next to Kipper's machine.

"What is it?" asked Spencer.

"It's the paper we'll use to print our newspaper," Nobby said.

"Why the sudden rush?"

Mavis put her arm around Spencer and explained. "If they've 'misplaced' some old machinery that no-one has used for a while, well, that's no big deal. But a whole reel of newsprint? That can only be used for one thing and that's to print a newspaper."

Kipper jumped down from his press. He unscrewed a couple of bolts from the side of the machine and lifted off a large metal door. He motioned for the men to slide the newsprint into the press.

"In here, lads," he said.

"Right,' said the Editor, firmly. "Let's get this show on the road. No more dilly-dallying! Kipper, we need to run a full test. Nobby, get out there and go cover a press conference, or something. We need content, people!"

"Will do," said Nobby. He threw his coat of his shoulder, grabbed Spencer by the arm and headed for the cavern door.

"Wait!" Red said. "Aren't we forgetting something?" Everyone stopped to listen. "How are we going to shift it?"

"Shift what?" Mavis said.

"The paper, of course. How are we going to sell the newspaper?"

"Ah," said Nobby, "for the answer to that question, we have to thank this young 'un." Nobby pushed Spencer front and center. "Go on, son. Tell them."

Red was incredulous. "You're kidding? We're going to trust him? We barely know him, right boss?"

"Just listen for a second," the Editor said.

"Oh, I'll listen," Red said. "Come on then, kid. How you are going to solve all of our problems? How are we going to sell our paper?"

Spencer shuffled nervously.

"We're not going to sell it," he said.

Nobby could not contain himself any longer.

"We're going to give it away," he said proudly.

At the rear of the cavern, a pin dropped. Red shook his head slowly.

"Well, thank you, Karl Marx and Spencer," he said. "Can we please have a serious suggestion? I thought the idea was to make some money."

"I think are they are onto something," the Editor said.

"What?" You believe this malarkey?"

"I know, I know," the Editor said, "but it makes some sense."

"Most newspapers make their money from adverts," Spencer said. "If we give the paper away, we can count our circulation as the total copies that we print rather than how many we sell."

"It's a numbers game, see?" chimed in Nobby. "The larger our circulation, the more advertisers will pay. If we don't sell many copies, we can't charge much, but if we give them all away, then every copy counts as a sale."

"How did you suddenly become such an expert on circulations?" Red said. "Last I checked, you were going write some gossip column or something."

"I ain't an expert," said Nobby. "I just listened to Spencer and Spencer listened to his dad.

"OK, then, geniuses. How are we going to give the paper away?"

"Don't worry," the Editor said. "For that, I may have a plan."

***

At the Scribe, the effects of the meeting with the Proprietor had reverberated around the office. On the news floor, The Scribe's editor had convened a meeting.

"Listen up, people!" he said. "If we can't get a handle on this one, we're as good as dead. I know we've had it easy but now we must put our noses to the grindstone, take our hands out of our pockets and pull our socks up."

The assembled group of journalists were not paying him much attention. They chatted among themselves, making cups of tea and reading the sports pages of other newspapers.

"You lot are my best investigative reporters. All you seem to be investigating are some of this street's more dubious hotspots. Let's get things rolling again, shall we? Get back on track with a full head of steam, eh? Let us try and find all this equipment, shall we?"

One of the journalists turned around and spoke to Mitchell, the new security chief, who had been lurking at the back of the room.

"Hey, Mitchell!" he said. "When I was a kid and something went missing, my dad would say he was going to close his eyes, count to 10 and see if it was returned. Can we try that?"

"One… Two…Three," chanted the journalists. Mitchell was unmoved.

The editor quickly became frustrated. "This is not a joke!" he shouted. "I have been reliably informed that we aren't the only paper in this town to be experiencing these phenomena. Not only has one of our old presses disappeared, but a source just told me that all the newsprint for the Sunday edition at The Tribune is missing."

"So, someone is sabotaging the competition," quipped a reporter. "What has that got to do with us? Boo hoo, right?"

Mitchell walked to the center of the office.

"All expense accounts are frozen until this is sorted out."

The office door banged shut.

"Wow, Mitchell" said the Editor, scanning the now-deserted room. "How to make friends and influence people."

5. A SCENT OF VICTORY

Nobby and Spencer stood at the side of a large room packed with reporters, notebooks at the ready. Nobby had made a brief attempt to clean himself up; he brushed his hair, washed his face, buttoned his cardigan — that sort of thing. He looked around and thought that he did not look that much different from anyone else there. What worried him more was being seen in a company of a boy. After all, this was no place for a child.

"Psst … Spencer," he whispered. "Go hide behind those curtains, will you? And make sure you take good notes!"

Spencer nodded and moved away. He hid in the folds of some drapes that divided the room just as a group of police officers walked to the lectern at the front. Immediately, the place erupted as all the reporters attempted to shout their questions at once.

"Wasn't the victim known to be having an affair?"

"Didn't the victim share a gym locker with the Honorable Member for Knightsbourne?"

"There have been rumors of a close relationship with a man of the cloth. Did you know about this?"

The police officer at the lectern vainly attempted to restore order.

"Please everyone, calm down! Does anyone have a sensible inquiry?"

His pleas went unheeded as the questions continued unabated.

"Commissioner, a source told us that the victim's shoes were covered in Mar…"

The rest of the question was lost in a wall of noise as everyone began to shout at once.

Eventually, the noise reached such a crescendo that the police officer shrugged, threw a bunch of press releases in the air and walked off. Nobby caught one and passed it to Spencer behind the curtain.

"OK. Let's go, kid," he whispered. "We're done here. Meet you outside."

Spencer shimmied along between the wall and the curtains until he reached a side door and slipped through. Nobby rode the tide of exiting humanity unnoticed, through the lobby and out the front door.

A nondescript man stood quietly at the rear of the room. He scoured the faces looking for something — anything — that did not fit. His eyes fell on the old geezer wearing the tea cosy with a press card stuffed in it.

Mitchell smiled to himself as he tracked Nobby out the door.

"Bingo!"

Outside, Nobby and Spencer hustled their way through the Christmas crowds. Once again, Spencer had trouble keeping up.

"Did you see that rabble?" said Nobby. "That's the kind of thing we want to avoid. You and I could do so much better than that, right? People want to know more than just: 'Were the victim's shoes covered in Mar …'"

Nobby suddenly stopped and, once again, Spencer plowed into his back.

Well, well," Nobby said, "look who we have here."

In front of them, a disheveled man played three-card monte on an upturned cardboard box. At some point, he might have been called dapper, but his grimy leisure suit had definitely seen better days. It was coupled with a flowery-but-now-faded shirt and a tie-knot the size of a child's fist. A battered trilby completed the ensemble.

A teenage couple handed the disheveled man some cash while a small crowd had gathered to witness the likely fleecing. Out of nowhere, Nobby bellowed at the man.

"Four of Clubs! Four of Clubs!" Spencer spun around in puzzlement. Nobby winked at him. "Four of Clubs … Northern Quadrant!"

The disheveled man quickly folded the cards into his coat and kicked the box into the gutter.

"OK, ladies and gentlemen," he said, "nothing to see here. Yes, sir, I do believe St Paul's is that way. If you get lost you should ask one of our wonderful police officers." He pointed a grimy finger up the street and shooed the young couple away. Then he caught sight of Nobby smirking at him.

"You mad beggar, Nobby," he said.

"Hello, Odds-On," Nobby replied. "Long time, no see."

"Yeah, well, I've been doing my research, ain't I?"

"Research on what, the bookies?" Nobby turned to Spencer. "Spencer, meet Odds-On, our sports reporter."

Odds-On smiled at Spencer. "Nice to meet you, son. Tell me, which card was the Queen under?"

"I'm not sure,' Spencer said. "The middle one?"

"Smart boy. Got any money on you?"

"All right, all right," Nobby said. "Hands off. Spencer is doing important work for us."

"Ah, so you're the young 'un I was hearing about from the lads. Welcome to the club, son. Are you sure you want to be a member?"

Nobby motioned for them all to hurry.

"Of course, he does. Let's move it. Odds-On, we are off to a meeting over by the docks. Are you coming?"

"Might as well. You've ruined my turf here. None of that 'four of clubs' malarkey, mind you."

"What was all that about?" Spencer asked.

"It's the lookout code," Nobby said. "An early-warning system, if you like. 'Two of Diamonds' means there is a tourist ripe for the taking. 'Ace of Hearts,' means, watch out, there are crooks nearby, likely to steal your earnings. 'Three of Clubs' means we can smell a plain clothes copper. 'Four of Clubs' means there's an imminent threat of arrest."

"I didn't see any police," Spencer said.

Odds-On smiled ruefully. "No, son. Nobby was having a joke. He knows that I've been working solo. Your friend is a proper comedian, ain't he?"

As the three moved down the street, two men who had been watching Odds-On's game peeled off and followed them at a distance. Mitchell whispered to his colleague, who then hurried over to a telephone box.

Nobby exited the docklands tube station and waved Spencer and Odds-On past. He craned his neck to look back down the stairs but there was no one there.

"Come on, you two. Hurry up!" said Nobby.

"Whoa," Odds-On said. "Ease on up there, cowboy. Where's the fire?"

"Mavis is waiting. I don't want her to wait on her own."

They rounded the corner, and in the distance, Spencer saw Mavis, Kipper and some of the others standing around an open fire in the wasteland. Mavis saw the group approaching and met them half way.

"How did it happen?" Nobby asked.

Mavis shook her head slowly. "Some soused ad manager, I think," she said. "Luckily, he doesn't know much, but he said enough. What's worse though, is that Caractacus has gone missing."

"Aye," added Kipper. "The cat is out of the bag, all right."

"What is going on?" Spencer asked.

"It seems one of our contacts in the wonderful world of advertising has told everyone about our plans," Nobby said ruefully. "And Caractacus — who was his contact — has vanished."

"Caractacus would never give us up," Mavis said.

"But Caractacus ain't exactly the smartest suit on the rack," Nobby said. "We need to be extra careful now, extra vigilant."

"Don't fret," said Kipper, winking at Nobby. "I've always got my secret weapon!"

Kipper grabbed the lapels of his rotting jacket and began to flap them vigorously.

"Kipper, don't!" pleaded Nobby. Kipper threw his head back and roared with laughter.

Kipper's expression froze, as his image was captured in mid-laugh by a telephoto lens.

"What's so funny?" asked Spencer, gazing up at Kipper.

"Hopefully, you'll never need to find out," Nobby said.

At the entrance to the tube station, Mitchell peered over the shoulder of his photographer.

"Make sure you get all of them, including the kid," he said. "I'll meet you back at the office after you've developed the photos."

"Don't worry, boss, I have them all."

"Careful!" said Mitchell. "They're coming this way!"

They turned to the ticket window and pretended to buy tickets as Nobby, Spencer, Mavis, Kipper and Odds-On entered the station and took the escalator down.

Two tube stops later, Kipper was planning his future.

"I'd like my own steam engine. No, wait, a steam train, with its own track. I'd give rides to everyone."

"I just want some warmth and security," Mavis added. "Nothing special, just somewhere where we can relax with friends."

"I'd buy my own bookies," sniffed Odds-On. He wiped a grimy sleeve across his face, grinning as he imagined all the hapless punters in his thrall.

"I thought the idea was that you'd all live in a retirement home," Spencer said.

"Or a race course," continued Odds-On. "Yes, a race course would be grand!"

"What do you want, Nobby?" asked Spencer. Nobby turned around to look behind him but did not reply, obviously distracted.

"Spencer asked you what you want to do if this all works out, dear," Mavis said.

"Oh, um, I always fancied owning a bingo hall. You know, on its own, clickity legs eleven, an' all that."

"What's the matter, dear?" asked Mavis. "Is something wrong?"

"Probably nothing. Come on, let's go this way." Nobby took a sharp left and darted down a smaller walkway. The others stopped, confused.

"But we can't get back that way, Nobby," Odds-On said.

"This way, I said!" hissed Nobby.

The others looked at each other for a puzzled second and then rushed down the walkway.

"Nobby, what is it?" said Spencer, running to catch up.

"Aye what's up? Do you smell something fishy?" Kipper asked.

"I think we're being followed."

"Really, dear? By whom?" Mavis said.

"I ain't sure yet, but better safe than sorry, right?"

The group turned the corner and walked down a small flight of stairs. Nobby stopped and turned around.

"Wait here for a second," he said. "I just need to make sure." He reversed up the stairs and peeked back around the corner. Mitchell and another man ran into view and stopped at the junction.

"Where are they?" asked the other man. Mitchell scratched his head as Nobby slowly withdrew from view.

"Not sure," Mitchell said. "But they can't be far."

Nobby tiptoed back down the stairs, only to find Odds-On with both hands clamped over his face, trying to suppress a sneeze.

"Oh no, no, no, no, no," wailed Mavis. "This isn't going to be good."

Odds-On could hold on no longer. He arched back and let rip a wet, messy sneeze that seemed to ricochet off the walls and echo down the corridor.

"That's torn it!' said Kipper. For one moment, everyone was quiet, listening for something that might signal that they had been discovered. They did not have long to wait.

"Move, move, move!" yelled Nobby, as Mitchell and his colleague skidded around the corner.

Everyone set off at a mad dash. They scampered down the corridor, turning at the end onto a station platform. Bobbing and weaving through a crowd of commuters, they sidestepped their way to another set of stairs at the far end.

"Keep going. Don't look back!" yelled Nobby, looking back to see Mitchell appear behind them.

The group arrived, out of breath, at a larger hall. In front, a pair of escalators took passengers up to the surface, while to the left and right, more tunnels directed commuters to other underground platforms.

"It's no good, dear," Mavis said to Nobby. "We can't lose them."

At the base of the escalators, two police officers chatted with passing commuters.

Nobby sighed. "I know. Listen, maybe I can buy you some time," he said. "Quick, take that tunnel and I'll make sure they are slowed down."

Nobby waited for Mitchell and his partner to appear in the hall. Nobby made sure the pair saw him. He smiled at them, then faced the officers.

"Oy, old Bill!" shouted Nobby. "Ain't you got nothing better to do than waste your time down here?"

The police officers turned to face their accuser.

"That's right," Nobby said. "I'm talking to you two bluebottles. Shouldn't you be out arresting someone?" He pointed to Mitchell. "How about that geezer? He just called you a plonker."

Mitchell slowly withdrew from a direct line of sight.

"Take it easy, grandad," the constable said calmly.

"Take it easy? Take it easy? Why, you whippersnapper, if I was your father, I'd box your ears."

Nobby staggered towards the men, feigning intoxication. Mitchell stared from a distance, watching the scene unfold. Nobby approached one of the officers and jabbed a rheumatic finger into the man's chest.

"And I still could! Used to box for the Navy, didn't I? Long before you were even spit in your father's whistle."

"That's enough, old timer," said the other police officer, a sergeant. "Move along."

"I'll give you, 'Move along!' said Nobby, growing more belligerent. "No respect! I could box all of your ears, I could."

"Maybe one day, sometime last century. But not now, whiskers," laughed the constable.

"Oh yeah?' Nobby gave one last jab with his finger into the middle of the constable's tunic while he swiftly bought his other hand up behind the officer and swatted the helmet off his head.

"Right, that's it!" said the embarrassed constable. "You're nicked!"

He attempted to manhandle Nobby but found him surprisingly strong. The sergeant — amused at first — realized he had to assist his younger colleague.

"Stop resisting!" he said as he tried to twist Nobby's arms behind his back.

"Ha! I ain't even started resisting yet," Nobby said.

The officers struggled to get Nobby to submit while they staggered around at the base of the escalator. Eventually, Nobby tripped the constable and held on to the sergeant before they all tumbled onto the escalator. As Nobby and the two police officers slowly ascended up to street level, Nobby turned and winked at Mitchell, who had witnessed the whole scene.

"Let's go," Mitchell said to his colleague. "The others have to be around somewhere."

Nobby's act gave the others some time to escape, but things had not gone well. They had chosen a corridor that ended at one of the few ancient lifts that hauled commuters up to street level. Odds-On pushed the call button repeatedly, while Spencer and Mavis nervously checked behind them, expecting Mitchell to appear at the other end at any moment.

"Come on. Come on!" pleaded Odds-On. "Is this thing working?"

"Where is Nobby?" asked Spencer. "What was he doing?"

"Don't worry about him," said Kipper. "If I know Nobby, he'll have a plan."

The light above the lift flickered on, a bell rang weakly and the door slid open.

"Thank goodness," said Mavis. "Hurry up!"

Odds-On pushed the metal gate aside and shepherded everyone inside. Mitchell rounded the corner at the other end of the corridor.

"Oy! You lot. Don't move!" he shouted, running down the corridor.

Inside the lift, Odds-On hammered on the button, while Kipper struggled to slide the gate shut. However, just as it was about to close, Mitchell inserted a size 10 boot in the gap between the gate and the wall. Without the gate fully closed, the lift could not move.

"Hello," Mitchell said. "What do we have here?"

"Dunno what you are talking about, mate," said Odds-On. "We're just trying to get home."

"Is that right? Can I give you a lift?" Mitchell smiled and beckoned his colleague forward. "OK, make sure you get all of them." He motioned for his colleague to photograph the group and then turned to face them. "You can take your time. We have all day."

Odds-On grabbed the bars of the cage and shook them, trying to dislodge Mitchell's boot. It would not budge. Kipper pushed Odds-On aside.

"Desperate times call for desperate measures," sighed Kipper. "Stand back, please."

"Kipper, no!" said Mavis. She pulled Spencer to the back of the lift, as far from Kipper as was possible.

"Don't fret," said Kipper, moving to the front of the lift. "It will all be over soon."

Kipper worked to undo the buttons on the numerous rancid layers of coats, sweaters and vests that comprised his clothing. Eventually, he grabbed the lapels of the outmost jacket layer and spoke to Mitchell.

"As my father used to say, 'This is going to hurt you, more than it will me.'"

"What are you going to do?" Mitchell scoffed. "Flap your wings and fly away?"

"In a manner of speaking, aye."

Holding the lapels of his jacket, Kipper repeatedly flapped them open and shut. After a few seconds, he threw his arms wide open and thrust his chest forward. Mitchell's colleague giggled at Kipper's actions. However, from deep within the disintegrating levels of Kipper's layered coats, something seriously rotten emerged — a smoky, greenish fog of war. Spencer could not see much as he sheltered behind Mavis, but he could make out Kipper flapping his lapels, encouraging the malevolent odor to curl towards Mitchell — whereupon it filled his nostrils and eyes with a festering, fetid fog. The whole corridor quickly became obscured by a noxious, burning cloud. Mitchell's eyes burned, his nostrils flared and his throat closed up.

"Can't ... breathe," he croaked, while his colleague fell to his knees, coughing uncontrollably. Eventually, Mitchell could take it no longer. He withdrew his boot from the gate and stumbled back up the corridor, hacking and gagging all the way.

With Mitchell's foot now removed, Kipper pulled the gate shut and Odds-On hit the 'Up' button one more time. The door shuddered shut and the lift rose out of harm's way.

When the lift opened at street level, everyone piled out at once, holding their noses and covering their eyes.

"Kipper!" Spencer said, "what was that?"

"Ooh, nothing for you to worry about," Kipper replied, grinning sheepishly. "It were just something I've been cultivating ... like a good bacteria, you might say."

The group nervously made their way across town, until they returned to the cavern. Kipper cracked open the heavy metal door and they all quietly entered.

"Are you sure Nobby will be OK?" Spencer asked.

"Oh yes, dear," Mavis said. "My Nobby will be just fine."

"Yeah," added Odds-On. "It's been ages since he had a night in the tank. Good sleep, a bit of breakfast. He'll be right as rain and out in the morning."

6. FRAMED

At The Scribe, five photographs — enlarged and covering the whole of one wall — dominated the Proprietor's office.

"So, let me get this straight," seethed the Proprietor. "Firstly, I am informed that over a number of months, large portions of our legacy printing paraphernalia have been purloined from under our protuberances."

"Say what now?" McKenzie whispered to Legal's Johnson, who pretended he had not heard and gently stepped away. Mitchell just shook his head.

The Proprietor marched over to McKenzie. His eyes blazed, his chest puffed and the buttons on his waistcoat almost popped.

"Someone's pinched our press, you prole!" he screamed. "and right from under our noses!"

He closed his eyes and took a deep breath to compose himself.

"So, that's firstly."

He walked around his desk and stared up at the photographs that Mitchell's partner had taken. Nobby, Spencer, Kipper, Mavis and Odds-On stared right back.

"And secondly, and frankly this is what amazes me the most, this is what causes me the utmost consternation: If this had been accomplished by a top crew of nefarious engineers, by a secret clan of special agents, or even — God forbid — by some of our more adept colleagues from the other side of Fleet Street, then maybe I would have been able to fathom it. But, no, we seem to have been victimized by — indeed, have been outsmarted by — no less than four bums and a boy!"

His voice rose to a crescendo. McKenzie cringed. Flecks of spittle flew past his face as the rant washed over him.

"There is a word to describe this situation," continued the Proprietor. "Two words actually. Firstly, Atomize. A-T-O-M-I-Z-E. 'To reduce to minute particles spread across a wide area.' Secondly, Nilpotent. A mathematical term, apparently. N-I-L-P-O-T-E-N-T, the definition of which I found eminently suitable for your predicament. 'Equal to zero when raised to some power.'

"You motley crew are supposed to wield some power in this town but you are not even equal to Jack Shandling, an idiot of a boy who works part-time sanding the burns off my secretary's floor. He has more common sense than the lot of you! You stand before me like a bunch of pathetic schoolkids caught smoking in the boys room, and yet you have the effrontery to tell me that a bunch of bums and a schoolkid have been stealing huge portions of our hardware with the intention of setting up a newspaper while we do nothing but contemplate our mastheads! Well, let me tell you something. If these low lives are not apprehended and brought before me within the next 24 hours, you lot will find yourselves reduced to small particles spread across a very, very wide area. Do I make myself clear? Do you understand?"

McKenzie, Johnson, and even Mitchell, nodded in unison.

"WHERE IS MY PRINTING PRESS?" he bellowed.

***

"So, we're going ahead with this plan, are we?" said Red, shaking his head. About 20 people had squeezed into the Editor's office in the Cavern.

"It's a done deal," the Editor said. "We should have thought of this before. If we sold the paper, then we'd need a way to collect the cash from all the vendors. That is too complicated, and we'd be easily rumbled. But if we give the paper away then we can get the ad agencies to deposit the money in an overseas account. It's almost untraceable, ain't that right, Bangers?"

"Right on, boss," Bangers replied. "It's a done deal, all right. The moment we told the media directors that we were giving the paper away and told them how many we were printing, they fell over themselves trying to place more ads."

"I don't know," said a skeptical Kipper. "I'm all for giving the paper away an' all. I just hope that my baby can handle the increase. That's a lot of papers you've asked me to print."

"We believe in you, Kipper," Mavis said.

"We do," the Editor said. "And we believe that you can do it by tomorrow. We go to press tomorrow night!"

"But, boss," Bangers said. "We ain't selling it, we ain't stuffing it through doors. How exactly are we supposed to give the flipping thing away? How will people even know about us?"

"Oh, they will know, all right," the Editor said. "Believe me, they will know."

***

McKenzie — still sweating profusely from his encounter with the Proprietor — slid into Harry's office at The Scribe. Harry, who had been scouring the jobs page of a competing newspaper, quickly threw the paper under his desk.

"You look rough," Harry said.

"I feel rough, McKenzie replied. "Bloody purgatory out there."

"Chicken supreme in the commissary?"

"I wish!" McKenzie said. "I'm just trying to keep a low profile for a few minutes. OK if I hide in here? No one comes in here, right?

"Help yourself," said Harry, ignoring the slight. McKenzie parked himself on the end of Harry's desk, and began to play with all his personal items: stapler; paperweight; framed family photo.

"Just because a couple of ancient pieces of machinery are absent from an inventory, suddenly it's all my fault," McKenzie whined.

Harry grabbed the photo from McKenzie and placed it back on this desk.

"Oh really?" he said. "A little birdie told me it was most of the MAX23512, two rollers, an inker, a stuffing machine and all manner of bits and pieces that had somehow gone AWOL. I wouldn't call that carelessness. No, more like incompetence, maybe. It may be a touch premature to suggest this but have you examined the jobs page recently?

Harry reached under his desk, straightened out the newspaper he had been reading and tried to hand it to McKenzie, who did not seem to be paying much attention. So, Harry put the paper on his desk and continued to rub it in.

"I hear they are looking for someone at Construction and Pre-stressed Concrete Quarterly," he said. "Let me have a word with their sales manager; we play cribbage together on Wednesdays. Perhaps I could put in a word for you."

"Yes. Could you? That would be nice," said a distracted McKenzie. He backed away from Harry's desk. "Well, thanks for putting up with me. Must be going."

"No problem," Harry said. McKenzie really was a strange fellow. Less than a minute ago, he needed sanctuary and now it seemed like he could not wait to get out. No wonder he was always drinking alone.

"Oh, one last thing," McKenzie. "I think I will have a look at that paper." He strode back over to Harry's desk and scooped up the crumpled newspaper.

"See you soon. Thanks again." McKenzie closed the door behind him.

"You're welcome again," said Harry, shaking his head in sympathy.

On the other side of the door, McKenzie's heart was trying to leap out of his chest. He opened the crumpled newspaper and withdrew the framed photograph that he had surreptitiously removed from Harry's desk. He did not know the slightly mousey woman with the pursed lips but he would never forget the face of the small boy who grinned next to her. Had it only been five minutes since a photograph of the same child had silently mocked him from the wall of the Proprietor's office? McKenzie stuck the photograph under his arm, dashed down the corridor, skidded around the corner and into the lift.

Later that afternoon, Harry was putting his coat on when the big red light on his desk phone began to flash.

"Must be a mistake,' he thought. "That light never goes off." He flicked the light casually to see if the bulb would extinguish. It did not and an insistent ring tone quickly accompanied it.

Two minutes later, the lift doors opened on the 13th floor and Harry tiptoed out.

"You can go straight in," said the secretary without looking up. "He's waiting for you."

"No one ever goes straight in," thought Harry. It was simply unheard of. He shuffled slowly through the double doors and looked around.

Inside, the Proprietor's office was almost as it had been the first time that Harry had been in it. That is, except for a large drop cloth that now covered one whole wall.

"Well, hello!" said the Proprietor, brightly, from behind his desk. "Sweetnum, isn't it? How are you today? How are things in the circulation department?"

"Um, good, thanks." Harry replied.

"I'm so glad to hear it. I hope that nothing is disturbing your reverie."

"I'm sorry?"

"I said I hope nothing is disturbing your beta rhythms, your leisure time, your somnambulance.

"Son ambulance?" Harry repeated. He was confused. What was all this about?

The Proprietor smiled and muttered to himself.

"Son ambulance? Yes, how apt. That's where he's going to end up."

He continued to address Harry. "I mean, I hope your job is going well … all things considered."

Harry, still confused, said what he thought the Proprietor wanted to hear.

"Well, penetration amongst AB1's is rising; figures show we're doing excellently in the suburbs; marketing tells us that more dog owners are reading us and TGI and urban stats are both encouraging."

"Good. Yes, that is encouraging."

The Proprietor stood up and walked over to the drop cloth that covered the wall.

"So, if everything is going so swimmingly," he said, his voice rising to another crescendo. "How do you explain this?" He ripped the drop cloth from the wall, revealing the huge photograph of Spencer.

"How do you explain this, you free-floating piece of flotsam! How do explain away the fact that this sprat, this shriveled fruit of your withered family tree has been stealing from me?"

Unsurprisingly, Harry was completely bewildered.

"But …I … That's my son!"

"Ten out of ten for observation. None out of ten for explanation!"

"What does he have to do with anything?"

"Let me spell it out in words of one syllable. No, that is not satisfaction enough." The Proprietor sat back down at his desk. He took a modicum of pleasure in composing himself and his next utterance.

"Listen and listen close. Your son is an enemy of the people, an enemy of the state. An agent provocateur, a quisling, a snake in the grass, a sociologist, a football manager, a TV chef, a game show host. He is the scum-riddled viper whose deadly venom strikes at the very heart of our beloved press freedoms!"

"But he's only 10!" pleaded Harry.

"By my reckoning that's old for scum. Most are just a dirty ring around the bath by then. Who is he working for, eh? The Font Mongers? The Ragamuffins? Below the Fold?"

"He walks his Nana's dogs, and he did a bit of gardening for Mrs. MacSheedy last summer."

The Proprietor stood up.

"Sweetnum! You are being either extremely dim or deliberately obtuse. I present evidence of your progeniture's malfeasance and you counter with horticultural obfuscation. Now, which one is it?"

Harry had no idea what the Proprietor was going on about.

"Dim, I guess," he offered. "But I don't understand…"

"The noblest pleasure is the joy of understanding," interrupted the Proprietor. "But you, Sweetnum, are not noble; you are wretched, with a capital 'Retch.'" He strolled over from behind his desk and fixed Harry with an intense stare that made him flinch.

"I am sure that if you brought your son to order he would happily explain all," said the Proprietor, trying a calmer tack. "Why don't you go home and have a quiet chat? Perhaps bring him back to the office so that we can clear this all up. I'll even provide the transportation and some company. I'm sure it's all one big misunderstanding."

"I suppose so," said Harry, still bemused.

Later that afternoon, Spencer padded down the path by the side of his house. Inside, the parlor curtains rippled. Spencer dipped below the window, tiptoed into the back garden and slipped inside the shed.

"Nobby!" he whispered.

"Right here, son," said a voice from the darkness.

"I'm so glad you're OK," Spencer said. "I was worried."

"About what?" said Nobby, rising from underneath a pile of newspapers. "About that malarkey with old Bill? Phht. What sort of investigative reporter would I be if I couldn't outsmart PC Rozzer and his band of merry men?"

"You're an investigative reporter, now?" Spencer asked.

"Well, I was just thinking. If this first article goes well, maybe for the next issue we could move up and do something more substandard."

"Substantial," corrected Spencer.

"Oh yeah, that's right. See what a good team we make?"

"OK, but we need to write this one first."

"Don't worry," said Nobby, tapping his temple. "I got it all in here; we just need to get it down on paper."

"OK," said Spencer. He stood up and made his way back to the shed door. "My Mother saw me coming home so I have to go and have my tea now, but I'll be back in a few minutes and we can start."

"Smashing!" Nobby said. "See you later." He snuggled back into his blanket of newspapers.

Spencer was surprised to see that his father was home, apparently waiting in the hall for Spencer.

"Oh, hello," Spencer said. "You're back early."

"Yes, I've been feeling a little off colour lately so I took the afternoon off," said Harry. "Besides, I thought it might be an opportunity for some quality father/son time. Anything to take my mind off this wicked indigestion that suddenly cropped up."

"OK," said Spencer, warily. This was new.

"I don't feel like we get to talk as much as we used to," Harry continued. "How is that project going?"

"Project?"

"Yes, the one you were doing on the newspapers, remember?"

"Oh, yes, of course. It went well. Thanks." Spencer was worried. His dad had never asked him about homework before.

"Can I take a look at it?" Harry asked. "What with me being in the business, and all."

Spencer thought quickly.

"It's being marked," he said.

"So how do you know it went well?" shot back Harry.

"I just have a feeling, that's all." Something was definitely wrong. Spencer thought he saw a sudden movement from the dining room. A chair scraped across the linoleum in the kitchen.

"I think I'm going to read in my bedroom," he said.

His father reached out and caught his arm.

"Wait," he said. "We haven't finished our talk."

"Ow, that hurts!" Spencer said. "What are you doing? Please, let me go."

Spencer twisted his arm and broke free from his father's grip.

"I'm sorry, son. I didn't mean to hurt you. It's just that …"

All hell broke loose as two burly men in suits ran out of the dining room right at Spencer.

"Get the little brat!" one of them yelled.

Spencer did not hesitate. He took the stairs two at a time, sprinted along the landing and into his bedroom, slamming the door behind him. He pushed his chest of drawers in front of his door and sat — panting — on his bed. Outside, the men began banging on the door. Spencer heard his father whisper to the men.

"Please, let me have a word, OK?" said Harry before calling out to his son

"Spencer. Please come out so we can have a conversation."

"I say we break it down," said one of the heavies.

"Spencer!" continued Harry, urgently. "Please come out before these men start damaging the house. You know your mother will hate that."

Still Spencer did not reply. A shoulder thumped against the door but it held firm. Spencer froze while his father plead with the men.

"Now gentlemen, there's no need for that."

"Stand back or you'll get hurt," an unfamiliar voice replied. Spencer was unsure if the men were talking to him or his father. Another crash against the door and their intentions were clear. Spencer, jolted into action, jumped off his bed, ran to the window and lifted the casement.

"Nobby!" he shouted. Another bang on the door and the chest moved about six inches. A hand reached in and tried to push it over.

"Nobby! Spencer shouted again, this time with more than a dash of panic. "Help!"

The shed door flew open and Nobby scampered out, sheets of

crumpled newspapers still lodged in his cardigan. He looked left and right, unsure as to where Spencer's voice had come from.

"Up here!" Spencer implored. "Help me. I think I'm being kidnapped!"

"What?" Nobby said. "Not on my watch!" The bedroom door opened another few inches and this time a full arm stretched through.

"Right," said Nobby. "Jump!"

Spencer was incredulous. "What?"

"That's right … jump! Come on. I was a Navy longshoreman for years. I caught all sorts of things in the Navy. Jump!"

"But Nobby!" he pleaded. He was hyperventilating now. The banging on the door had increased and he could see one of the hinges was working loose.

"Son!" Harry implored. "Please open the door! Everything will be all right, I promise."

Spencer looked to his bedroom door, then down at Nobby in the garden below and then back to his door.

"Trust me, boy!" shouted Nobby, his arms open wide.

Spencer's mind was made up after one more thump on the bedroom door. He edged through the window frame and onto the sill. Nobby spat into his hands; rubbed them together and braced himself for impact. Finally, the bedroom door gave way and the two heavies rushed in. They paused for a second and looked around before running to the open window. Below them, a small boy was lying atop a spread-eagled old man.

"Damn!" said one of the men. They dashed back out of the room and along the landing, past a bewildered Harry.

Outside, Spencer jumped up quickly. Nobby took a few seconds longer.

"I 'spose I never had to catch nothing moving in the Navy," he said, rubbing a shoulder. "Help me find my glasses, will you?"

"Hurry! Let's go!" said Spencer. He picked up Nobby's glasses, now bent more than ever, and placed them over the old man's ears. He took Nobby's good arm and pulled him to his feet.

"This way. Come on, they'll be here soon!" he said.

They ran down the garden path behind the shed. Spencer pulled a couple of wooded slats from the fence and they slipped through. A moment later, the two heavies appeared at the back door of the house. They looked up at the open window and then at the empty space where a couple of seconds previously their quarry had lain inert.

"Where are they?" said one of the men.

"Obviously, not here!" said the other. "You go that way." The pair split up. One ran over to the front of the house while the other examined the shed and the back garden. He nosed around but could not find anything until he peered over the wooden fence into the neighbour's back garden. There — disappearing through the begonias — was his quarry.

"Got you!" said Heavy #2. For a big man in a tight suit he was quite nimble, vaulting over the fence, then hopping over an ornamental pond. However, he had underestimated both Spencer's local knowledge and Nobby's country-craft. Fifteen minutes and one missing loafer later, he had almost given up when he saw a tea cosy peeking out from a house farther down the street. Nobby quickly ducked back in the hope that he had not been rumbled. He pushed Spencer around another corner and put a single finger to his lips. As the footstep approached, Nobby held his breath.

Spencer held his breath also, but for different reason. As he had pressed himself back against the wall next to the front door, the door opened and a massive, hairy hand reached out. It completely covered Spencer's mouth. A second hand reached out and grabbed Spencer by the shoulder, and pulled him inside.

The house was dark and Spencer's eyes took a few seconds to get make out the large figure in front of him. His nose however, was quicker to react.

"Kipper!" Spencer whispered, his voice cracking with relief. "It's you! Thank goodness!"

"Right ye are," said Kipper. "Hang on while I grab Nobby." Kipper cracked open the door and pulled Nobby inside.

"You two are in trouble," Kipper said.

"Yes, my father knows everything,' said Spencer, still a little out of breath. "He's got these men chasing after us."

"Och, don't worry about them," replied Kipper. "No, you are in trouble with the boss. Nobby hasn't written anything yet. It's deadline day and there's a hole in the paper where his article is supposed to be."

"No need to worry on my account,' said Nobby, winking at

Spencer. "I'll have it later today. It just needs some of the rough edges knocked off it."

"Looks like someone was trying to do that to you pair," Kipper smiled. "Let's get us out of here. How hard can it be to lose these numbskulls?"

Kipper shepherded Nobby and Spencer through hallway and into the darkened living room. He peeked through the curtains and then motioned for everyone to go through to the kitchen.

"Bye dear. See you same time next week," came a woman's voice from the living room sofa.

"Aye love, will do," replied Kipper. Before Nobby and Spencer could pause to see who the voice belonged to, Kipper had steered them through the door and outside. They scurried alongside an unkempt hedge and out into the street.

A megaphoned voice stopped them in their tracks.

"That's far enough!" One of the Heavies stepped out from behind a parked van and pointed a finger at them.

"Do not move!" he bellowed through the megaphone. Nobby looked around to see which way offered the best chance of escape. Kipper, however, had no intention of escaping.

"You know the drill, son," he whispered to Spencer. "Get behind me." Kipper began to unbutton his jacket again.

"Stop!" yelled the Heavy. Kipper ignored the instructions and walked towards him, unbuttoning.

"I said, 'Do not move!'" This time the Heavy was not quite so assertive. He backed away from Kipper and moved behind the van.

"Now, sonny, you don't have to be afraid of me." Kipper smiled and kept walking. Mitchell appeared around the front of the van.

"How true!" he shouted. "OK. Now!"

The rear doors to the van were thrown open, and two men dressed from head to toe in chemical warfare suits — complete with gas masks and rubber boots — jumped out. They carried large fire extinguishers that they pointed at Kipper. One billowed smoke while the other sent a ribbon of foam straight at him.

Kipper did not stand a chance. He was still fumbling with his buttons when the blast hit. It coated him in a thick layer of white foam, knocking him to the ground. He spluttered and struggled as the smoke and foam filled his mouth and eyes. He felt helpless to resist as numerous muscular arms tossed him into the back of the van.

Amid the smoke and confusion, Nobby pulled Spencer over a garden wall and the pair ran alongside a fence and away to safety. In the distance, they heard the van doors slam shut. The throttle revved, the tyres squealed and off it drove, creating yet more smoke. Mitchell emerged coughing from the haze.

"One down, two to go," he said, smiling. His confidence was short-lived however. There was no sign of the vagrant and the small boy.

Half an hour later, Nobby and Spencer emerged separately from the Embankment Tube station. It was getting dark now and the wind had picked up again. They sidled over to a bench overlooking the Thames. Nobby sat down at one end of the bench, Spencer at the other. After a couple of minutes of silence and avoiding each other's gaze, Nobby glanced around.

"OK, I think the coast is clear."

"What are going to do?" asked Spencer, nervously. "They've got Kipper."

"He'll be fine," Nobby said. He checked all his pockets, searching for something. "Kipper can look after himself. And if he can't, then we have people who can."

"But he's your best friend!"

"I know son, but we can't worry about that. We'll tell the others in a couple of minutes and they'll have a plan to help Kipper. They probably know already. We have a pretty good bush telegraph, you know." Nobby stroked his beard and winked at Spencer.

"Right now, we need to concentrate on the matter at hand."

"What's that?" Spencer asked. Nobby scooted along the bench to get closer.

"Helping me, of course."

Spencer's brow furrowed. He looked up to see Nobby smiling at him and holding up a battered HB No. 2 pencil and notepad.

"That's right!" Spencer said. "Nobby's Diary. Let's get started."

They hunkered down around the notebook. Spencer quickly transcribed Nobby's directions onto paper — occasionally asking him questions, erasing errors and underlining important passages — until they were done.

"There. That's smashing!" remarked Nobby after Spencer had read the piece back to him. "Not bad for a pair of outlaw scribblers on the run. Something we can be proud of."

"I'm not sure I'd say proud," Spencer said earnestly. Nobby would have none of it, though.

"Proud, yes of course I'm proud. It is cutting-edge, is what it is. It's Now. Fresh, if you like."

Spencer made a face. "If you say so," he said.

Nobby noticed night was drawing in. "It's also late," he said. "We need to move."

Spencer, looked at his wristwatch. "It's only 5."

"No, not 'late' late," Nobby said. He stood up waved the notebook in the air. "I mean 'deadline late.' If we don't get this over to the Paper immediately they'll have my guts for garters."

Nobby slid the notebook into a pocket and stood up.

"Chop, chop, then. Let's go," he said.

"What's a garter?" Spencer asked as they walked to the Tube station.

"I think it's some kind of sock." Nobby lifted Spencer over the turnstile.

"How can they do that?" Spencer continued as they descended the escalator. "How can they make your guts into a sock? That's just strange. Aren't guts supposed to make you brave? 'That guy had a lot of guts,' they say. So, if you make his guts into a sock, does he still have enough to be brave? I don't know Nobby, it's a strange saying, don't you think?"

"Beats me," Nobby replied. "We will ask Mavis. She knows all about that kind of stuff."

"I think, I'm going to need all my guts, thank you very much."

***

Nobby cracked open the door to the Cavern and he and Spencer entered. They stood on the balcony and marveled at the scene below. Everywhere they looked, people were busy: typing reports; filling giant ink baths; moving heavy objects from one spot to another, a veritable hive of enterprise. Frantic activity everywhere, except for the printing press itself. Caution tape lapped the giant machine that squatted silently in the center of the room.

"Finally!" shouted the Editor from across the room. "The prodigal son has returned to grace us with his presence." Everyone stopped what they were doing and stared up at Nobby and Spencer.

"This seems familiar, right?" Nobby said out of the side of his mouth.

"Yes, it does," whispered Spencer. Nobby cleared his throat and addressed the throng below.

"Boss, bad news, I'm afraid. Kipper was …"

"Yes, yes," interrupted the Editor, dismissively. "We know. He's fallen into enemy hands. We're working on it." He walked quickly up the stairs and pushed his face close to Nobby's.

"My question to you is, 'Do you have it?'" he asked quietly.

"Of course," Nobby replied. He produced the notebook from his pocket and handed it over with a flourish.

"It's late," said the Editor.

"It has to be last minute," Nobby said. "What use is a diary column that is a week, or even a day old? No, it has to be hot. It has to be now!"

"It has to be here and it has to be good," said the Editor. He opened the notebook and began to read. Spencer thought he saw a hint of the Editor's lips moving, but he could not be sure. When he had finished reading, the Editor closed the notebook and tossed it down to a minion.

"Here, go type that up," he said before turning back to Nobby. "Not bad, not bad at all. It's a little superficial and doesn't really plumb the depths like I'd hoped for, but it's a good start. Well done."

Nobby breathed a sigh of relief and surreptitiously squeezed Spencer's shoulder.

7. NOT-SO-FRIENDLY-FIRE

Kipper's shoulders had also been squeezed, but in a far less caring manner. Although the windows in the minivan windows were blacked out, he had figured out where he was going from the detritus of discarded twine and yesterday's newspapers that were his companions. They came to a halt and he heard the metal door of a loading dock rolling up. The van doors were flung open and Kipper was blinded by the mega-watt glare of a pair of construction lights. Another blast from a fire extinguisher left Kipper coughing and spluttering. Two hazard-suited heavies picked him up under his arms and frog-marched him towards a lift at the far end of a corridor. One of the men produced a key from under his hazard suit, inserted it into the security slot in the lift and pressed the button for the 13th floor.

Arriving at the secretary's anteroom, Kipper was immediately escorted into the Proprietor's office. The giant photographs of Nobby and the rest of the crew had vanished from the walls, replaced with various architectural drawings and plans for what looked like a wartime bunker: concrete blocks with tall fences and tiny windows. Kipper found them fascinating and studied them intently, so much so that he jumped when the Proprietor stood up from behind his desk. His voice boomed out across the room.

"Good evening, my good man. How are you?" he said jauntily. "I've been dying to meet you. It is rare that I get the chance these days to entertain others in this publishing enterprise. One gets so caught up in running one's own ship that there is a tendency to lose track of what others in the Fleet are doing, don't you agree?"

Kipper frowned; he had no idea what the man was talking about.

"I don't know about any ships. Nobby is probably your man there."

"Nobby, eh? Mitchell. write that name down." One of the heavies that had manhandled Kipper into the room flipped up his gas mask. It was Mitchell. He fumbled for a pencil, while the Proprietor continued.

"One never loses track of what flotsam or jetsam is though, don't you agree? And I think we both know what piracy is, don't we?" Finally, he noticed Kipper examining the plans.

"Ah, I see you are admiring my flagship. That is to be my battleship, my destroyer. This will be the ultimate weapon in the destruction of rival mastheads. A totally automated production center. Electronic news gathering, simultaneous reporting and deadlines, direct invoice processing. This could be a completely new media. No more problems, no more journalists, no more unions, no expense accounts, no accountants, no lawyers ... no other egos. No one between me and my public."

"And nowhere for us to sleep at night," Kipper said under his breath.

"What was that?" the Proprietor asked, annoyed that his ruminating had been interrupted. Mitchell piped in.

"He said that the new facility wouldn't have anywhere for them to sleep at night."

"Did he really?" The Proprietor looked at Kipper. "And where are you currently domiciled?

"Huh?"

"Where is your abode, your residence, your place of habitation?" Kipper still blanked.

Where do you lot live?" screamed the Proprietor, slamming his fist on his desk.

Kipper understood now and nodded his head slowly.

"Ah, wouldn't you like to know?"

"Indeed, I would sir, but all in good time," said the Proprietor, calmer again. He walked from behind his desk and looked Kipper up and down.

"Mitchell, you can leave us now. Go and do some research on our friend 'Nobby.' I'd like a few words, mano a mano, with this gentleman."

"I don't think that is a good idea, sir," replied Mitchell. Unseen by Kipper, he flapped the lapels of his jacket, trying to catch the Proprietor's eye.

"Oh tosh, we're just going to have a little chat, him and I. You can wait outside, if you must."

"But sir ..." implored Mitchell.

"Out, I said!"

Mitchell and the other hazard-suited heavy sheepishly withdrew to the secretary's office. The Proprietor paced around his office until he was standing behind Kipper.

"I know that you have purloined various printing artifacts with the intention of publishing a periodical. I can help you. I have years of experience in most of the required fields, you know.

"Well, if we ever think of doing something like that, we'll be sure to reach out," said Kipper, fumbling under his coat. A button popped off one of his jackets and rolled across the marble floor.

"In fact, I think I may be able to set you up with something in my organization if that might suit you."

Suddenly, Kipper spun around to face the Proprietor, thrust out his chest and threw open his coat.

"Never!" he bellowed. "I'll never work for the likes of you."

Once again, the putrid fog of war sprung from under Kipper's clothing, filling the room with a soupy brew of stale acridity and fetid humidity. Sunlight that had been streaming through a skylight was extinguished, leaving the two protagonists merely as silhouettes in a sweaty box.

Kipper flapped his lapels, directing the evil haze at the Proprietor. Before long, the stink reached his nostrils. As the Proprietor vanished into the growing murk, Kipper thought he saw him close his eyes and breath in, slowly and deeply.

The next thing Kipper heard was the tear of Velcro, the squeak of latex and the smooth rrrrip of a zipper, quickly followed by the Proprietor's voice.

"You poor, poor thing. You had no idea, did you?"

Kipper felt a wave nausea wash over him as his own rancid tendrils were forced backwards by the Proprietor's own emissions, mixing with something that neutralized his own malodorous scent. Clouds of noxious gases poured over Kipper, like stormwater flooding a sewer. He felt his throat close up and his eyes burn as something foreign — yet familiar — entered his air passages. Unable to see or breathe, he fell to his knees, coughing and spluttering, rendered helpless by the power of the Proprietor's own foul stench.

"Not a fan of these effluvia emanations, eh? Not too clever now, are we?"

The Proprietor walked towards Kipper, with almost a spring in his step.

"It's been such a long, long time since I released my own secret weapon that I almost forgot the pleasure it can bring."

The Proprietor bent down and whispered in Kipper's ear. "Not-so-friendly-fire, right?"

He let that sink in before walking back behind his desk and sitting down.

"Do you have anything to say now? Any nugget of information that you'd like to pass on?"

Kipper — still on all fours — could only manage a hacking cough.

"Maybe you'd like a little more time to consider your position, now that you are in receipt of more pertinent information."

The Proprietor pressed a big button on his desk. The skylight swung open and an extractor fan funneled the funk up and out of the office. He pressed the intercom button.

"You can come in now," he said. The double doors to his office swung open and Mitchell — still wearing the hazard suit — entered cautiously.

"Our friend here requires a little more time to consider his options," the Proprietor said. "Would you see to it that he is offered our usual hospitality?"

"Of course, sir," said Mitchell, motioning to his colleague to assist him. They picked Kipper up off the floor and carried him out of the office. They pushed past the secretary, who was waving the cattle prod enthusiastically.

"Will it be 110 or 220 volts tonight, sir?" she said.

"Not tonight, unfortunately."

Two floors down, Kipper — his eyes still watering and bloodshot — stumbled along another corridor, pushed and prodded from behind by Mitchell and the other heavy.

"Ish Room 11-20?" said the heavy, although the mask made his question almost unintelligible.

"Take that off, you dimwit!" Mitchell barked. "Yes, it's always Room 1120." Mitchell gave Kipper another poke with a broom handle, directing him around a cleaning cart that blocked part of the corridor.

A cleaner was on her knees, picking up the remains of a take-out dinner discarded on the carpet outside the office door. She placed the plates and cups in one plastic bag and scooped up the discarded food with a dustpan.

"Out the way," Mitchell said.

"Ooh, sorry, luv," replied the cleaner. "Almost done."

Mitchell pushed past and stopped at Room 1120. It had a sheet of paper on the door that read, "Office Closed for Decorating." Mitchell jiggled the door handle but found the room locked.

"Damn," he said. "No one tells me anything!"

The next door was locked, too.

"Excuse me, dear," the cleaner said. "This office here is open. I just finished cleaning it."

Mitchell looked into the office. It was windowless except for a skylight.

"This will have to do, I suppose." He faced Kipper. "Get in here, and wipe that smile off your face. You've got nothing to smile about!"

"I'm not smiling," Kipper said. "I'm just trying to catch my breath."

Mitchell prodded Kipper into the room and shut the door, locking Kipper inside.

"Stand guard here." he said to the heavy. "And don't let anyone in or out!"

Mitchell turned to go, almost tripping over the cleaner again.

"What the …"

"Ooh, I'm sorry dear. How clumsy of me." she said. "I'm done now, though."

Mavis stood up, but kept her head down. She collected her plastic bags and her brushes, put them in the cart and pushed them down the corridor.

Inside the office, Kipper put his feet up on an empty desk and waited. Soon, the skylight opened and a rope ladder descended. A few seconds later it was followed a pair of old boots connected to greasy trousers, a substantial rear end and a familiar voice.

"Don't rush me. I'm getting there, ain't I?" Nobby stage-whispered to an unseen accomplice above him. "Blimey, you'd think we was all in the SAS, or something."

Kipper steadied the rope ladder with his foot, as Nobby came down, followed quickly by Red. Odds-On waved from the skylight above.

Nobby looked around the office. "This is a bit of a pickle, mate," he said to Kipper.

"Aye, and you've not heard the half of it! You'll never believe it when I tell you!"

"Ain't got time for that now," Nobby said. "We need to get you out of here and back to base." He surveyed the office and casually opened a file cabinet. "Although…" He paused.

"Wait a second, wait a second. What's all this?" Nobby pulled out a manila folder and examined it closely. In it were some papers marked 'Private' and a few photographs.

"Ooh," Nobby exclaimed. Red leaned in for a quick peek.

"Ooooooh," he said.

"There's loads of this stuff," Nobby said excitedly. He rifled through numerous other folders, all containing photographs and/or papers. "We could use this," he said. "It's a bloomin' goldmine!"

He picked out one photo and showed it to Kipper, who winced. "Ooh. That's not right."

"No, it is definitely not," said Nobby, rotating the picture. "And as a sitting QC at the Old Bailey, you'd think he'd know that." Nobby opened more and more folders, creating a growing stack on the file cabinet.

Red opened a drawer on the next file cabinet. "There's more here," he said.

"Psst!" hissed Odds-On, from the skylight above. "Come on, you lot; we've got to get out of here, pronto."

"Red, Kipper, you go first and I'll hold the ladder," Nobby said. As they climbed, Nobby surreptitiously stuffed a few folders into the waistband of his trousers.

The foursome quietly made their way across the rooftop. They opened a fire door on the roof of a neighbouring building and took the stairs down to the street below.

Spencer and Mavis waited nervously in the shadows of a narrow alley. They were overjoyed when they saw the men approaching.

"Kipper!" Spencer said. "You're OK!"

"Never better," said Kipper, ruffling Spencer's hair. "How did you find me so quickly?"

"We just followed our noses," Nobby said.

But Red wanted to know, "Did you tell them anything?"

Kipper stopped. "Are you kidding me?" he said, incredulously. "You'd ask me that?"

"Sorry, sorry." Red said. "I was told that we needed to know."

"I'll tell you what you need to know," said Kipper, his eyes suddenly ablaze. He hitched his thumb over his shoulder, pointing back at the newspaper offices.

"You need to know that the Big Cheese back there is one of us!"

"What do you mean, 'One of us'?" asked Red.

"Well, not like all of us, but he's more like... me," said Kipper pointing to his midriff. Still, they did not get it.

"He has a rare, but useful talent."

Finally, he shrugged in exasperation and began unbuttoning.

"Wait, Kipper. Stop!" everyone cried in unison. Mavis was aghast.

"You don't mean?"

"Aye, I do mean."

"No, no, no," Nobby said. "That can't be. Are you sure?"

"As sure as eggs is eggs."

"I would have taken good money on that not being so." said Odds-On.

"Then you would have lost your shirt, my friend."

The group headed down the alley, and as they turned the corner, Spencer ran to catch up with Kipper.

"Hey! What happened back there?" he asked.

"I don't want to talk about it," said Kipper quietly. "The only good part is that I don't think anyone else knows, not even his staff."

"Nobby thought about this for a few seconds.

"Wait!" he said. Everyone stopped in their tracks except Spencer, who once again, careered into Nobby's back.

"No-one else knows, eh? That's good," said Nobby. "Let's keep it that way."

Red shook his head.

"This is important stuff," he said. "We have to tell the others."

"I don't think so," said Nobby. Who knows how they would react? Everyone is so wound up right now, what with publication being so close"

Kipper nodded. "You may be right, Nobby. No need to rock the boat."

Nobby turned to Mavis.

"What do you think, love?

Mavis carefully considered the question.

"You know me, I like being straight with everyone, but I can't see how it would hurt us not to share this for a couple of days. At least until we get the first edition out."

Odds-On nodded sagely. "I'm OK with that."

"Agreed then?" said Nobby. "We keep this just between us at least until we publish?"

Red raised his hand.

"Er, that's like tomorrow," he reminded everyone.

"Sweet Heart of Midlothian!" exclaimed Kipper, clapping a hand to his forehead. "That's right! We need to get back now!"

Kipper accelerated down the alley and turned onto a main street. The holiday crowds parted for him like a hot knife through rancid butter.

"This is it, then?" said Spencer to Nobby, as they attempted to keep up with Kipper.

"Yep, tomorrow's the big day, all right," he replied. "Exciting, ain't it?"

The Proprietor was not quite so excited when he heard that Kipper had escaped.

"Children!" he yelled. "I'm literally dealing with children." Mitchell stood at attention nearby.

"And who on earth has heard of anywhere in this place being redecorated. Ever?"

"I did think it was a little odd at the time sir, what with it being Room 1120," Mitchell said.

"You thought it was odd, did you?" fumed the Proprietor. "Odd that someone might be redecorating an office in a building that we're moving out of shortly? Odd that you, our supposed Chief of Security, were unaware of the fact that 1120 was closed? In what universe does that make sense?"

Mitchell shuffled his feet uncomfortably.

"Let me remind you of something."

"What might that be, sir?"

The Proprietor pressed the call button on his desk and the double doors to his office swung open.

"I don't get 'odd,' Mitchell, I get even."

"Yes, sir," said Mitchell, quickly backing out past the incoming secretary.

"Ah, my dear," said the Proprietor. "Would you please be kind enough to bring me some personnel files? While we might not be in the business of redecorating, I think now is a good time to clean house."

8. FREE BIRD

There was total silence in the cavern. No one moved and only a few breathed. Thirty men, women and a single child gazed up at the giant machine that dominated the room. Kipper, an oily rag draped over his shoulder, stood on the machine's platform, a key in his hand. He brought the key up to his face to examine it carefully. He nodded, seemingly satisfied, and inserted the key into its slot on the control panel.

"Here we go," he said, turning the key. It made a soft clicking sound but nothing else. A collective gasp rose up from below and floated to the ceiling.

"What's wrong?" said Nobby, climbing the ladder up the side of the machine.

"Uh oh," Kipper said. He tried again. Click. Nothing. And again. Click. Nothing.

"Hmm." Kipper rubbed his chin thoughtfully.

"Och, that's right! I have to push this button as well!" Kipper's face broke into a mischievous grin as he pressed the large button next to the key. The machine coughed once and then sprang into life, filling the cavern with a low, steady rumble.

"Kipper!" said Mavis, laughing. "How could you?"

"Sorry. I couldn't help it. The look on all your faces!"

"You darn well near give me a heart attack, you begger!" said Nobby.

Tension mounted as the designated hour approached. The Editor's fuse had been particularly short. He dashed from one task to another, barking orders at the staff as they hurried to meet their deadlines. Eventually, he climbed up to the balcony and summoned everyone.

"I know this has been a long, hard, journey," he said. "But no one should forget why we got into this in the first place. This city is harsh and unforgiving; its inhabitants are cruel, its public buildings, its transportation system and its department stores are forbidden to us. The shelters are dangerous, the soup kitchens basically serve gruel and our law enforcement officers offer us little or no protection."

The Editor warmed to his speech, encouraged by numerous exhortations of, "You got that right," and "Ain't that the truth!" from the crowd below.

"And yet, we knew that there was always Fleet Street. It was always somewhere we could come back to, somewhere where we wouldn't stick out. It may be a bit thread worn, a bit down-at-the-heel, but hey, that's why it suited us so well. Maybe it was that bottle of lager to be found with a few last sips… maybe the remnants of a catered lunch brought back from a Covent Garden brasserie."

Nobby smiled in recognition and squeezed Mavis's hand.

"And the warmth. Oh, the warmth! Once those presses started rolling every night and all that lovely hot air wafted through the grates and onto the pavement, well, I don't have to remind you."

The Editor's voice had become more and more strident, but now he paused for effect.

"And *they* want to take that away from you. If *they* had their way, The Street would turn into a place as cold as the new steel towers on the edge of town that they covet so much. They would forget the traditions, the history, the *life* of the place. Therefore, we have to act. All we want is some warmth and companionship, and it looks like The Street can no longer give us that."

He walked back down the stairs towards the press holding aloft a printing plate.

"But this, this can provide the warmth we need. This can provide us with warm nights with feather mattresses, toasty blankets and soft pillows." With great ceremony, he handed the plate over to Kipper.

"And so, ladies and gentlemen, it is with no little sense of irony that I announce that we can put this first edition to bed!"

A cheer went up as Kipper climbed the ladder onto the printing press platform. He turned and saluted the crowd below. He inserted the final printing plate into the machine. He fiddled with some dials and turned some wheels. He cleaned a dirty valve with a rag and reinserted it into its socket.

"One moment," said Kipper, suddenly appearing a little nervous. He scratched his head and went over to the rear of the platform. No one could see what he was doing but there was a good deal of hammering and some mumbled swearing. Finally, Kipper reappeared, looking flustered. He pulled out a large collection of keys from a chain around his neck and — after looking through them all carefully —selected one.

"Here we go," he said, turning the key.

It seemed to Spencer that the printing press was almost alive. It wheezed, it shuddered, it rumbled and squealed. The noise was deafening. Kipper pushed a large lever, releasing a blast of steam. The Cavern shook as the machine gathered pace. Gears engaged, cogs turned and cylinders rotated. Everyone cheered as the newsprint fed through the machine where it was printed, cut, bundled and deposited on the floor of the Cavern as a fully formed stack of newspapers.

The Editor picked up a bundle and held it above his head.

"Welcome to the first edition of The Daily Bread."

"That's a flippin' miracle, that is!" Nobby said. He did a little jig of joy each time a bundle of newspapers rolled off the press. A group of men divided the bundles into two piles. They loaded one pile onto a rail cart positioned near the tracks in the tunnel. The other was stacked next to the balcony.

The Editor kept checking out the clock on the wall.

"Keep 'em coming, no dilly dallying!" he cried. "Time is money, and we don't have much of either!"

"Hey, boss," asked Red. "Why are we splitting them up?"

"Ah, the cart is for national distribution," said the Editor, smiling for the first time that evening. He pointed to the stack by the stairs. "But we have something special for this lot!"

***

Harry sat at the bar of a pub around the corner from his office. On the stool next to him was a torn plastic bag that held two framed pictures, a chipped mug, a small cactus and a stapler.

The pub was filling up with the after-work crowd and a man squeezed in next to him.

"Is this yours, mate?" he said.

"Huh?" Harry said distractedly.

"This bag. Is it yours?"

"Oh yes, sorry." Harry replied, moving the bag onto his lap. The man ordered his drink.

"No wristwatch?"

"Excuse me?"

"No wristwatch, paper weight?" said the man, pointing to the bag. "It looks like this was your last day."

"Yeah, it was. Ten years I'd been working at that place." Harry reached into his pocket and waved his dismissal papers.

"At least they let you clear your office," said the man. "They wouldn't even let any of us back into the Scribe building."

"You're from The Scribe too?" said Harry. "Sorry, I didn't recognize you."

"Not surprising … night shift," the man said.

The bartender lined up a couple more drinks.

"On the house," he said. "Celebrating your new-found freedom."

Harry thought about this.

"Yeah, why not? I should celebrating, right?"

Harry lifted his glass.

"To my son," he said. "After all, it's not every day that your son becomes a newspaper publisher."

"Wow," said the bartender. "You must be very proud."

"Oh yes," Harry said. "Very."

∗∗∗

It was nearly midnight when 20 men pried open the security door of a dark basement and squeezed through. There was much huffing and puffing as feet were stepped on, ribs were elbowed and personal space invaded. All carried large bundles slung over their shoulders.

"Hell's bells!" chirped Nobby. "Why do we have to do it this way? What's wrong with the lift?"

"There hasn't been a working lift in this building for years," replied the Editor. "No power, neither. These stairs is the only way up." He lit a match so that the others could follow him. "Besides, it's not like we want to broadcast ourselves."

The fading light thrown by the match led the group to the bottom of a staircase that spiraled up, around a corner and out of sight. The men reluctantly began the climb, single file.

"Remind me to veto any attempt to add any Sunday Supplements," wheezed Nobby.

"Stop your whining!" Kipper said from somewhere below. He tried to push past some of the other climbers, but was blocked at every attempt.

"I can take some if you like," said Spencer who was right behind Nobby but had nothing to carry.

"Please. Can't a geezer have a bit of a moan without consequences, these days? I'm fine, I can carry my weight, don't worry."

"Pipe down, you lot," whispered the Editor. We can't afford to get nabbed now. You're going to need every last ounce of breath for the stairs."

He was right: One hour, countless floors and many extended rests later, Red opened a fire door and peeked into a large room filled with catering tables and stacked chairs. Large sheets had been thrown over a pair of sofas and a bar — albeit one devoid of liquor or any consumables — gathered dust at one end of the room. A set of double doors led to a deserted kitchen; the only illumination was external, a dim glow from London's lights, twinkling through the epic windows that encompassed the room from floor to ceiling.

"OK. Coast is clear," Red said. The men staggered through the door, threw their packages down and collapsed in a heap. It took a full 15 minutes for the stragglers to arrive, Nobby and Spencer among them.

"Can't … we … make … this … a … monthly?" he wheezed.

"Where are we?" Spencer asked, looking around.

"You'll see when it gets light," Nobby replied. "For now, you need to get some kip. We've a big day tomorrow."

Spencer yawned.

"I am rather tired," he said.

"Yeah, just rest your noggin on that lot," said Nobby, pointing to the bundles. "You'll soon get used to it." Spencer nodded and made his way over. He lay down and tried to get comfortable.

"Psst." Someone was shaking Spencer by the shoulder. He tried to roll over but the shaking continued.

"Wakey, wakey, matey!" Nobby's throaty whisper gently roused Spencer from his slumber. "Rise and shine; we have work to do."

Spencer sat up and stretched. He rubbed his eyes, not recalling for a moment exactly where he was.

"Move it, sunshine. This is the big day."

Now he remembered. He looked around and saw Red, Kipper and some of the others, unpacking the bundles. Standing up, he was shocked to find himself looking down at the London skyline. The sun was rising in the east, basking Tower Bridge and the Thames in a shimmer of watery light. Spencer turned around … and around. There were no walls, just 360 degrees of glass.

"Nobby," he said. "Is this the …"

"GPO Tower," interrupted Nobby, smiling broadly. "It used to be the Post Office Tower; not sure what they call it now." He followed Spencer around as they surveyed the whole of London stretched out below them. Big Ben, St Paul's, the South Bank.

"Of course, it's empty now, has been for years. This used to be the restaurant. London's finest dining, so I'm told. Kings and queens; ambassadors and bankers; tycoons, magnates and moguls. You name it; they've all polished off a Beef Wellington up here."

Spencer frowned. "Beef Wellington?" he said.

"No, I've never had it, neither," Nobby said. "But how good can it be if it's named after a boot?"

"What are we doing here?

"In a way, this was your idea," said Nobby. Spencer was startled.

"I don't think so," he said. "I would have remembered."

The Editor strolled over and smiled.

"Our esteemed Diary Columnist is correct," he said. "We have you to thank, young man, for planting the seed by which this idea could germinate. After all, was it not you who suggested that we give our paper away for free?

"Well, yes, because that's what my dad says is the future."

"An astute forecast, I am sure," continued the Editor. "So, that is what we will do. We will give them away for free. Come on boys, open them up."

A few of the men moved around the room, opening the latches on the windows. They pushed on the top half of each window, forcing the bottom half to hinge in. A cold breeze immediately whistled through the room.

"Help me unpack these," said Nobby, holding up one of the hessian-covered bundles. Spencer grabbed the twine and untwisted it until the hessian fell clear. Nobby held the stack of the newspapers tight to his chest. He was beaming.

"Here we go!" he said. "Wish us luck!

Spencer looked around and saw all the men holding multiple copies of the newspaper. Red was even scanning through it.

"Boss," he asked, quizzically. "Did you read this?"

"Read what?" replied the Editor, impatiently. "Yes, I read it, of course. Why?

"Turn to Page 6."

There was a rustle as everyone turned to that page.

"Page 6 is the diary page," said the Editor. "It was the last one I proofed because it came in late."

"That's my page," said Nobby, proudly. "It looks great, doesn't it? I hoped it would make an impact"

"It has certainly done that," Red noted.

Spencer opened the paper to Page 6.

"It's backwards," he whispered.

Groans filled the room. The Editor held the paper open. His knuckles were white; his face was red but his language trended towards blue. He let flow a stream of invective that sailed through the open windows and out into the ether.

"Kipper!" he shouted. "You put that last plate in back to front!"

Spencer turned the paper around to show Nobby. The whole page was printed backwards. The headline was backwards, the body copy was backwards, the various adverts were back to front. It was completely illegible, aside from the photos, which — although one could not immediately tell — likely were backwards, too. "Nobby's Diary" now read "yraiD s'ybboN."

The Editor walked over to Kipper. Kipper towered over the much-shorter man, but Kipper flinched a little as the other approached.

"I gave you that last plate to put in the press and you put the bloody thing in backwards," the Editor said through gritted teeth.

"You don't know that, "said Kipper, on the defensive. "You may have set it up wrong. Those things are very confusing. My job was to get the press up and running. Your job was to give it something to print."

Nobby was crestfallen.

"But, but …" he stammered. He slumped back against a wall and stared at the page. Spencer sat down and tried to console him.

"Nobby, It's OK. We'll make sure we get the next one right. And, think about it, we can reuse some of the same content again. Or maybe even write some different stuff."

"Who said there was going to be a next time?" murmured Nobby, shaking his head. "I put everything I knew into writing that column."

"Well …" said Spencer.

"Boss," interrupted Red, pointing in the direction of the approaching daylight. "It's getting late."

"Yes, yes," said the Editor, leafing through the other pages of the paper. "Look, it's only Page 6 that is backwards. There is nothing we can do about it now. We'll just have to continue as planned."

He marched around the room like a general boosting the morale of his troops.

"OK, zero hour is approaching. Everyone knows what to do, yes? A minor setback, that is all. We will still give 'em what for, right?"

Eventually, he approached Nobby and crouched down beside him.

"Listen, I'm sorry. These things happen; we just need to make sure that they never happen again."

"That's easy for you to say," Nobby said. "You're not the one whose name appears above 20 column inches of complete, bloody rubbish. I'll be a laughing stock."

"The Editor thought about this for a second.

"Firstly, no one knows who you are, so you are not likely to be a laughing stock. Secondly, no one can read it anyway, so as far as I can see you are in the clear. Pull yourself together and come give us a hand."

Reluctantly, Nobby offered it and the Editor pulled him to his feet.

"We have a newspaper to distribute," said the Editor. "Time to upset the apple cart!"

The papers were stacked by the windows and each pile had a man attending to them. The Editor stood on a chair so everyone could see him.

"Listen up, people. This is the sharp end, right now, right here. Things are going to be different from this moment on. If we stick together, if we stick to the plan, then we can walk away with everything we wanted."

There was much nodding of heads and various 'Yeahs!" from the assembled men.

"Ready then? On my mark …"

Nobby pulled Spencer over until they stood in front of the only unattended pile of newspapers.

"Sorry," said the Editor, pausing. "One more thing. I'd like to thank Her Majesty's Royal Mail for providing us with this magnificent venue and therefore helping us with our delivery today."

A cheer went up again.

"Three … two … one … Go!"

All around the room, people threw the newspapers out the windows. Some even sat down and tried to shove their entire stack out with their feet.

Spencer looked on aghast.

"What are you doing?"

"What does it look like?" replied Nobby. "We're publishing, ain't we?"

"But you're throwing them away!"

"Given the complete fiasco of my contribution, I'd say that might be a good thing, but, no, not at all. It's blanket distribution, is what it is. What did you think we were doing up here?"

"I don't know…this is the Post Office Tower and he just thanked the Royal Mail, so I thought maybe we were giving them papers and letting them deal with it."

"Oh, no," said Nobby. "This is far more efficient. Come and give me a hand."

Spencer paused, then shrugged and grabbed a handful.

"Ok, why not?" he said.

Spencer leaned over and threw everything he had out of the window. Then he pressed his face against the glass to watch.

The wind caught the papers and spun them around. They whirled and twirled, twisted and soared. Some floated delicately downwards, like jellyfish gracefully descending into the depths of an ocean. Others zipped and zoomed like streamlined paper airplanes. Still more tumbled downwards gracelessly, as if trying to get to street level as quickly as possible. Viewed from a distance, a casual observer might have thought a flock of birds — having made the tower their home — had taken to the wing, startled by some silent trigger. Spencer thought they looked beautiful in the dawn light.

The men were captivated also. They watched as the papers drifted down, down —until most were out of sight. A calm settled on the men in the tower; they reflected peacefully on the scene laid out below… That was, until the blare of the horns interrupted their reverie. Car horns, van and bus horns, and in the distance — but approaching rapidly — police horns.

"That's our signal," said the Editor. "Time to make ourselves scarce. Back to the Batcave!"

Any semblance of serenity evaporated as the men bundled through the fire door, down the spiral stairs, out of the basement and into another maze of Tube corridors. Nobby however, grabbed Spencer by the arm and broke away from the group.

"Come on," he said. "Let's take a look-see."

At ground level, there were newspapers everywhere. They had floated onto the streets; into coffee bars and through office windows; down into the Tube Stations and on park benches. Curious commuters had already begun to pick them up and read them.

Spencer scooped up a handful and threw them joyfully in the air, only to have them caught by a breeze and blown across the road. They wrapped around the helmet of a passing motorcyclist who had been walking his bike through the congested street.

"Oy! Watch what you're doing'!"

"Ooh, sorry!" said Spencer, moving away quickly.

Traffic was at a standstill, a mix of the usual rush hour snarl and this highly unusual paper chase. The loudest horn blasts originated from a large, black limousine that futilely attempted to pass other vehicles.

"What on earth is this all about?" demanded the Proprietor from the back seat. He peered through his tinted windows, unable to discern the cause of his delay.

"Get out now and see what's happening," he said to the chauffeur.

The chauffeur tried to open the driver's door but it would not move more than a couple of inches—hemmed in by another car stranded in a sea of stationary vehicles.

"Come on, man. Hurry up!"

"I can't sir. We're stuck," said the harried chauffeur. "We don't seem to be going anywhere soon."

"That's ridiculous," replied the Proprietor. "Let me have a…"

Without warning, there was a thump across the front of the car as a few copies of the newspaper landed on the bonnet. Other sheets from the The Daily Bread drifted down and spread themselves across the windshield. The Proprietor learned forward to see what had caused the commotion. His eyes narrowed as he made out the headlines splayed across the glass.

"Get rid of them!" he screamed.

The chauffeur made another panicky attempt to exit the car but the space was still too narrow for the door to open. He wound his window down and tried to grab the papers off the windshield but his arms were too short. As a last resort, he turned on the windshield wipers, but accidentally hit the windshield washers, rapidly transforming the sheets into paper maché and the glass into a gummy, opaque mask.

A few more pages then floated in through the driver's side window and landed quietly on the Proprietor's lap. He took another deep breath, shook his head and closed his eyes.

***

A few miles away, on a suburban railway station platform, a vagrant slept as a train pulled into the station. The freight car door opened and bundles of newspapers were thrown onto the platform. The vagrant waited for the train to pull away before he withdrew a large, hessian bag from under his bench. He walked over to one of the bundles of newspapers, removed their receipt slip and pushed the papers off the platform where they fell into some nasty-looking undergrowth. He slipped the receipt under a twine knot on the replacement papers and went back to his bench, keeping one eye open to ensure that they were collected by the local agent; just like any other morning.

***

88

Nobby and Spencer tumbled into the Cavern through the metal door and surveyed the room before them. The place was buzzing. Phones rang, fax machines chattered and bottles of cider were clinked in celebration. Kipper was atop the printing press, a can of oil in one hand and a transistor radio pressed against his ear in the other. Odds-On, Shoulders and Mavis gathered around an ancient television, also checking for any coverage of their morning glory. Everyone was bubbling with enthusiasm. Everyone but Nobby. He scanned the room distractedly.

Spencer had unsuccessfully attempted to cheer him up on the way back to the Cavern. Mavis also noticed that something was not right.

"What is it, dear?" she asked.

"Oh, nothing."

"Nobby!"

"You know what it is. Everyone is celebrating, but it seems like I'm just wasting my time. On the way back over here, we saw hundreds of people picking up the paper and reading it. You know what I saw? Page 6's lying in the gutters, or in rubbish bins, loads of them. No-one was picking them up and reading them."

Mavis took Nobby's hand.

"Come over here, dear."

She led Nobby over to the television set and squeezed past Odds-On and Shoulders. Spencer followed, curious to find out what was going on.

On the screen, a journalist was reporting from outside the Post Office Tower. The camera cut away to show some children running around collecting the various pages from The Daily Bread, putting them in the correct order and then offering them for sale for a few pence.

"Young entrepreneurs!" said Odds-On. "We've only been at this for a morning and we've already got a Youth Training Scheme."

The camera cut back to the reporter —who also held a copy.

"Turn up the volume," said Mavis.

"*... and it was here, around six-thirty this morning that a new concept of what might be termed 'guerilla publishing' was literally launched onto an unsuspecting public ...*"

"Cheeky git," said Odds-On.

"*Unabashedly appealing to the lowest common denominator in all of us, the paper is an amalgam of improbable lies, half-truths, gossip, rumor and sleaze. Plus, of course, Your Stars."*

"It's nice, an' all," said Nobby. "But what's it got to do with me?"

"Wait, dear. Look closely"

"There has obviously been a great deal of market research conducted prior to publication. With more on that, I'd like to bring in our research and analytics expert, Geoffrey Smalls. Geoffrey?"

The camera zoomed in on a well-dressed man with slicked back hair, serious spectacles and a frivolous bow-tie.

"Thank you, Helen. While their distribution system is clearly unique, the real hook that has fascinated both public and professionals alike was the reverse printing of the Diary page which seems — if I'm reading this correctly -- to have been written by someone called 'Nobody.'"

"That's not Nobody," Spencer exclaimed. "That's Nobby!"

"That's me!" agreed Nobby, astonished.

The camera cut back to the men reading the paper. They were trying to read the Nobby's column by holding up the paper and reading it from the reflection in the shop window.

"One can only speculate — who are these people's publishers, and what are they trying to say? One thing is for sure, they have certainly tapped into a populist nerve."

The television panned over to show two older women leaning over a parked car. They held the paper in front of the side mirrors, again, trying to read the copy, which now displayed correctly.

"That's tosh, that is," said Shoulders, dismissively. "It weren't nothing but an accident."

"Accident or not, your career seems to have been resurrected, Nobby," said the Editor who had been watching from outside his office but had quietly approached the television.

"Thank you, Geoffrey. We'll have more on this still-breaking story during the evening news."

Nobby did not move.

"You can breathe now, dear," Mavis said, gently pushing Nobby's lower jaw shut.

"Well that's a turn up for the books, ain't it?" he beamed. "Who would have thought it?"

***

Later that morning, Spencer's mum heard the front door bell

ring. She put down her cup of tea and turned to her mother.

"Who could that be at this time of the morning?"

"Careful, Denise," replied her mother. "You never know these days."

"Oh Mother. Not in this neighbourhood. We have community policing now."

Denise walked down the hall and opened the front door. Her husband — disheveled, hungover and possibly still a little inebriated — stood before her."

"You!" she exclaimed.

"Who were you expecting? Aristotle flippin' Onassis?" Harry said.

"Actually, I thought it might be our son. He's almost never home now and who knows what he's been getting up to."

"Oh, I have a pretty good idea," Harry said.

Denise's mother had followed her into the hall.

"He's been drinking!" she blurted, peering out from behind her daughter. Harry leaned on the doorframe to steady himself.

"To paraphrase my previous employer, 'Ten out of ten for observation. None out of ten for perspiration.' … or something like that."

"What do you mean 'previous employer?' You'd better not have a new job without asking me. Does it come with a car? Is that what you've been celebrating this time?" Denise said.

"Hardly," Harry replied. "I was celebrating the fact that I no longer have the means to support you."

"What?"

"That's right, light of my life. I am no longer gainfully employed, so unless Mr. and Mrs. Jones have also been sacked, there is no point in keeping up with them."

"Don't you 'light of my life,' me," said Denise, reaching behind the door for an umbrella. "We've still got two more payments on the washer and dryer! Get out of my sight and don't come back until you do get another job!" She gave Harry a swift jab with the point of the umbrella and slammed the door shut.

"… and it better be a good one too!"

Denise marched back into the kitchen.

"I warned you," said her mother. "Right from the beginning, I said…"

"Be quiet, mother," snapped Denise. "Go get the gin."

***

Nobby spent the next few hours basking in the warming glow of his new-found fame. Initially, this had had been awarded by his fellow workers at The Daily bread, but after Nobby had made a couple of trips around the Cavern and had shaken everyone's hand at least once, he decided to seek affirmation further afield.

"Psst," he whispered to Spencer. "Let's get out of here,"

"Where are we going?"

"I thought we might hit the streets, get a feel for how we're being received out there."

It did not take them long to find out. As Nobby and Spencer crisscrossed the myriad passageways and alleys around Fleet Street, they discovered that the news had traveled fast. Recessed doorways contained either sleeping homeless or concerned press executives holding furtive conversations outside — unable to speak freely with their colleagues in their offices above. If a doorway had a sleeper in it, Nobby would surreptitiously remove a copy of their newspaper from under his coat, and gently lay it over the vagrant, making sure his column was front and center. If he saw a pair of executives examining the contents of the newspaper, he would walk back and forth in front of them, attempting to discern their reaction. Spencer frequently had to pull him away before the executives became suspicious, reminding him that he was supposed to be incognito.

It was not long before Spencer was exhausted.

"Can we *please* take a break?" he implored.

Nobby looked up from rescuing a couple of copies of The Daily Bread from a rubbish bin. To the casual observer it might have looked like he was ferreting around for a discarded beer can, but in reality, he was smoothing out the crumpled papers so he could recycle them back into a viable newspaper.

"Hmm? A break? This is fun though, ain't it?"

"It was," Spencer replied, "about an hour and a half ago."

Nobby paused. He leaned on the edge of the rubbish bin and thought for a moment.

"I 'spose it wouldn't do no harm," he said. "And besides, it's about time we thought about our next column."

"Next column?" Spencer said. "There's going to be another?" Nobby rubbed his chin.

"Do yer have any money on yer?" he asked.

"A little."

"Good."

Nobby pointed towards a dingy café down at the far end of the street.

"That place over there is the greasiest of greasy spoons. I've been meaning to give it a try when the opportunity presented itself."

Nobby and Spencer sat in the café, an empty mug of tea and a glass of water in front of them, and planned Nobby's next column.

"How many of these are we going to do?" Spencer asked. "I thought it was a one-off and then you go somewhere warm?"

"That was the idea, but you have to be flexible in this business," said Nobby. "It turns out that things are far more expensive than we thought."

"This *business*?" said Spencer.

"I know, I know," Nobby acknowledged. "But can't an old geezer like me have a bit of a dream?"

Their waitress approached the table. A cigarette hung from her lip. She picked up the empty mug in front of Nobby.

"Do you need anything else?" she asked.

"Not right now, love."

"I hope you know what you are doing," said Spencer.

"Of course," Nobby replied. "We just make stuff up and the punters read it."

The waitress circled back around. "If you don't mind, can you finish up?" she said. "I've got others waiting for the table."

"Hold your horses," Nobby said, "this is an important business meeting we're having." The waitress removed Spencer's water and vigorously wiped the table clean with a grimy rag.

"Maybe hold it in the executive boardroom then. I can't retire on a cuppa and a glass of water."

"Ooh, snark-ee!" said Nobby, rising from the table. "You can forget about your tip."

Spencer smiled nervously, fumbled for some change and put it on the table. They left the café and walked down the street.

Nobby looked back at the café. "That waitress wants to be careful, she does," he whispered to Spencer. "She might find herself in the newspapers, if you catch my drift." He winked at Spencer. Spencer did not think it was funny.

"Hey, hey! What's wrong? I was joking."

"Nothing."

"Someone has a hair in their marmalade. What is it?"

"I've been thinking," Spencer said. "Can't we write about other stuff? How about cartoons? They're fun."

"This is fun."

"Are you sure?"

Nobby sighed and sat down on a retaining wall. He patted the wall and Spencer parked himself next to him.

"You should understand, these are public figures. What is known as 'fair game.' They have two personalities, public and private. The public one is the one that's offered to the press — and we can have fun with that one — and we try and leave the other one alone."

"It doesn't feel right, that's all," Spencer said.

"You'll get used to it. It's like rubbish collection. At first, it may reek, but you remind yourself that you are doing a vital service to the community. Pretty soon it smells as sweet as a rose."

Nobby reached under his coat and pulled out one of the documents that he had taken from the office where they had rescued Kipper.

"I mean, look at these Herberts; they are just asking for it. Some of this stuff might even have some truth to it." He turned the file around so he could make out the one of the photographs more clearly and then put it under his coat before Spencer could see.

"Maybe not that one, but there are plenty others. Come on, if we knuckle down, we can bang this out before teatime."

By the time Nobby had finished dictating the column — while sneaking looks at the stolen files and Spencer reluctantly reading them for him — it was getting dark.

***

The Cavern was still full of people working on the next edition. Nobby blew a kiss over to Mavis and then walked over to the Editor.

"Here you go, boss," he said. "Backwards again, please!"

"Ah, Nobby," said the Editor. He handed the column back to Nobby without reading it. "Give it to me later, will you? I've been trying to reach you, Come on into my office."

Nobby passed the column to Spencer and motioned for Spencer to follow him.

"Hang on to this for me, would you?" Nobby said. "Better safe in your hands than sorry in mine."

"Actually, I just wanted to speak to you," said the Editor to Nobby. He turned to Spencer. "Thank you for all your work and advice, but I think now might be the time to say goodbye."

Nobby's reaction was immediate and extreme.

"Whoa. No! What are you saying? We owe so much to Spencer, here. If it wasn't for him, we'd have no idea how to get the paper out there and now you want to cast him off like he barely existed?"

Spencer shrugged and turned to leave.

"It's OK," he said quietly. "I should be going, anyway."

"Well it's not flippin' OK with me!" shouted Nobby.

The Editor was confused by Nobby's reaction.

"What's all this about?" he said. "The boy should be getting back to his home, that's all. We don't want a missing persons' report, do we? When were you last home, son?"

"It's been a while." Spencer acknowledged. The Editor pointed over to the phone bank.

"Go call your parents and let them know you're OK. Then Kipper needs some help, I think."

Spencer looked over to Nobby, who nodded in agreement.

"Yeah, that's not a bad idea," he said. "Sorry boss, I'm a bit wound up."

"You ain't kidding," said the Editor. "We need to talk." The Editor closed the office door behind them.

Spencer phoned home but his Gran picked up.

"Your mother's sleeping." she said. "I'm not going to wake her, with what she's been through."

"Tell her I'm staying over at a friends' tonight, will you?" Spencer said. In the office, some kind of argument was going on, but he had no idea what it was about.

"Could you pass the vice grip, laddie?"

Spencer could hear Kipper's voice but he could not see him. He circled the press until he found Kipper on the far side, entwined around some particularly complex gearing.

"What are you doing in there?" Spencer asked, handing him the nearest large tool.

"No, the vice grip, not the rethreading adapter." Kipper said. "Now watch closely, laddie. I'm going to teach you all about the gear differentials. This could be a lesson that will open up whole new vistas of career opportunities. This one here is the main drive shaft which links with the motor and the exhaust manifold."

Spencer passed Kipper what he hoped was the vice grip.

"Once I've made these adjustments, I'll have her purring like a wee kitten. Last time we only got her out of second gear, next time we'll really open her up and see what she can do!" Kipper leaned out of the machine and saw that Spencer's attention had drifted away. Nobby had left the office and was coming over.

"What is it?" Spencer said.

"He's nuts," said Nobby, pointing in the direction of the Editor.

"It's too big an opportunity to miss," said the Editor, who had followed Nobby across the Cavern floor.

"He wants me to do a talk show!" said Nobby. "Me. On the telly!"

"What do you know about television?" Mavis asked.

"I mean, I watch it, don't I," Nobby replied. "Can it really be that hard?"

"You'll get caught," said Spencer. "Can you trust them?"

The Editor tried to reassure them.

"It's all above board," he said. "They promised he'd be a 'surprise guest,' No one else knows he's going to be on. They said he can wear a disguise if he likes."

"How did they ever find us in the first place?" Nobby said. "And how do you know they won't follow us back here?"

"We'll be careful, that's all," said the Editor. "Imagine it, Nobby. On television, being interviewed by Helen Hanson, no less."

"You're not seriously considering this?" Mavis said.

"I don't know," said Nobby, stroking his beard. "I suppose I might, if it were going to be handled properly."

***

The buzzer on the Proprietor's desk sounded.

"Mr. Mitchell is here, sir," the secretary said. "Should I send him in?"

"Ah, yes, please do," the Proprietor said. Mitchell sidled in cautiously, wondering if this was his exit interview.

"Don't worry," the Proprietor said. "I still require some degree of participation from you and your ilk. For the time being, you still have gainful employment at this establishment."

Mitchell relaxed a little — now that he knew he was not getting the sack.

"You wanted a report, sir, on how the vagrants escaped?"

"Yes, indeed, that would be tremendously useful information. Go ahead."

"It seems they may have had someone on the inside, sir, because a redecorating sign on the door to Room 1120 was faked."

"Brilliant deductive capacity, Mitchell. An interloper, eh? Anything else?"

"Well, yes. They used a rope ladder and a skylight."

"I see."

"And one more thing," said Mitchell. "There seem to be some files missing from that room."

"Really?" The Proprietor studied the ceiling. "And what, pray tell, was in those files?"

"Pretty ugly stuff, actually. Stories that we've shelved because Legal told us that even we can't print them."

The Proprietor strolled around his desk, his thumbs jammed into his waistcoat.

"So, what you are saying is that *if* someone decided to print those stories, they could be in serious trouble? The ramifications of such malevolent defamation would undoubtedly draw the immediate ire of the legal profession's most ravenous minds. Is that what you are saying, Mitchell?"

"Yes and no, sir."

The Proprietor stopped in his tracks. He had anticipated what Mitchell's answer would be, but this equivocation was unexpected.

"What do you mean, 'yes *and* no'? Make up your mind, man!"

Mitchell cleared his throat, uncomfortable with the news he was about impart.

"I mean, 'Yes, if they were to publish those files, they would clearly open themselves up to all kinds of libel action."

"And 'No?'"

"No, if they published them backwards again, sir."

"What?"

"It's really quite clever, actually," said Mitchell, warming to his explanation. "Legal says that if these stories <u>were</u> printed back to front, then *legally* it's nothing but gobbledygook. Each reader would have to decipher and interpret what — and who — it is being written about. Because it isn't in English or any discernable language, then quite possibly it can't be libelous."

The Proprietor sat down with a thump.

"So, what you are saying is that these arrivistes, these upstarts can print anything they want, about anybody they want, and there's nothing anyone can do about it?"

"That's what Legal says," said Mitchell.

"Well, well, well," he said. "It seems that I might have underestimated our friends."

The buzzer sounded on his desk and the secretary's voice came over the intercom.

"Phone call on your private line, sir. It's a Miss Hanson."

The Proprietor shooed Mitchell out the door.

"OK, that will be all for now. Do not wander too far. I may require your services."

He waited for the door to close and then picked up the phone.

"Helen, my dear. How *are* you?"

***

Nobby was very uncomfortable in his new clothes.

"No natural fabrics here, I'll bet," he said, inserting a finger under a starched collar in an attempt to loosen it. Spencer tugged on the sleeves of the tweed jacket that had ridden up to Nobby's elbows.

"It's a bit tight," he said.

"I know," Nobby said. "It's all they had at the thrift shop. But look, it's got leather patches on the elbows like what a real writer might have."

Spencer backed up to take a better look. Nobby stood before him: jacket bulging and buttoned; tie askew; trousers sagging.

"How do I look?"

"I suppose it will do," Spencer replied.

"You don't sound very sure,"

"I wouldn't call it a disguise. It's still you, just in different clothes," said Spencer, trying to be constructive.

"Ah, but I haven't added my piece de resistance," Nobby said brightly. He removed his knitted hat and replaced it with an enormous flat cap that he pulled down tight, so that most of his face was in shadow.

"And last but not least …"

With a flourish, Nobby reached inside the breast pocket of his jacket and produced a pair of wraparound sunglasses. He breathed on each lens, rubbed them on his sleeve and then placed them over his wire-rimmed spectacles.

"Not bad, eh?" he said, striking a pose.

"I'm over here," said Spencer.

Nobby spun around to face him.

"Sorry, it takes a while for my eyes to adjust. These lenses are pretty dark."

"It's definitely different," said Spencer. "Let's take it for a stroll."

Spencer threw all of Nobby's old clothes into a shopping bag. He popped the latch on the door and guided Nobby out of the department store fitting room. A mother and daughter who had been waiting in line to use the fitting rooms, suddenly changed their minds.

Spencer steered Nobby through the store, aisles brimming with holiday shoppers, until they made it to the street.

"Are you sure you want to go through with this?" said Spencer. "It seems a big risk to take."

"The reward could be big, too," Nobby said. "It's great publicity, and if we want to maintain our initial impact and increase readership nationwide, then our responsibility is to participate in ventures such as these."

"Stop it," said Spencer. "Who told you to say that?"

"You're right," agreed Nobby. "That's not me."

"Just be yourself. Explain how you got here and why you are doing this."

Spencer picked a piece of lint from Nobby's lapel. Nobby took a deep breath.

"Of course. Wish me luck."

Spencer looked around. He had not realized that their path had taken them in front of the TV studios. Outside the main door, an audience line had begun to form.

"Whoa," Spencer said. "You can't go in through the front. We have to go around to the back entrance, remember?"

Spencer pulled Nobby by the arm and they made their way down an alleyway by the side of the building. Spencer rapped three times on an old stage door, battered and chipped with peeling paint. After a few moments, the door opened and a surly-looking production assistant leaned out.

"Yeah?" he said.

"I'm Nobby," said Nobby.

The assistant checked his clipboard and waved him in. He looked down at Spencer.

"And you?"

"Excuse me?" said Spencer. The plan had been to enter separately so that Spencer could check out the lay of the land.

"Are you two together?"

"Er, no."

"So, who are you?"

"I'm nobody," Spencer said finally.

The assistant took one final drag on his cigarette and flicked the butt past Spencer's ear.

"That's right, kid," he said, retreating into the gloomy interior and letting the door swing shut. Spencer blinked for a couple of seconds and then backed up the alleyway where he stood in line with the rest of the audience.

Nobby tried to take in as much as he could but there was simply too much happening. A swarm of twentysomethings — resplendent with headsets, clipboards and stopwatches — directed the traffic flow inside the studio. He followed the production assistant to a swinging door marked 'Makeup.'

The assistant pointed to a barber's chair.

"Sit there and when you're done, come to the green room."

Before Nobby could argue, ask or even react, the assistant turned full circle and marched on to his next assignment.

Better do as I'm told, Nobby thought, making himself comfortable in one of the chairs. It was a full 10 minutes before anyone approached.

"You're talent?" asked a gum-chewing makeup woman who burst into the room. Her blouse was hidden underneath a plethora of hair-styling clips, combs and brushes that hung around her neck.

"Thanks," Nobby said bashfully.

The woman smiled at him as if he were a child. Nobby noticed that more combs protruded from her voluminous 'do' in at least three different places and she held in her hands numerous puffs, brushes and Q-tips.

"No, love. You're on the show tonight?"

"That's right."

"So, what do you need?"

Nobby was confused but tried to play along.

"What have you got?"

"A couple of options. Redford or Roger Moore are the basics."

Nobby gave up.

"I'm sorry, you've lost me," he said.

"My job is to make you look presentable on TV. Most of our first-time guests ask if I could make them look like someone famous."

"Bobby Darin," Nobby said quickly. "I always thought Bobby Darin was a good-looking geezer and I loved 'Mack the Knife.'"

"OK, that's a first," the woman said.

She went to remove Nobby's cap and sunglasses but he pushed her away.

"On second thoughts, I think I'll stay as I am, thanks," he said, rising out of the chair and making a dash for the swinging doors. He looked for a sign to the green room, whatever that was. In the distance, he heard the woman shouting at him down the corridor.

"Bob Hoskins! I can do a half-decent Bob Hoskins."

Meanwhile, Spencer had slipped through a door onto the balcony of the studio set and was watching the audience file in. To his astonishment — seated among the tourists and students who would normally constitute a daytime talk show audience — Spencer saw Mitchell and two burly associates. They sat two-thirds of the way back from the stage in aisle seats, conspicuous in their dark suits. Mitchell fiddled with something in his ear.

"I knew it!" said Spencer. "I knew it was a trap." He tried to think of a way to warn Nobby, but before he could react, the house lights dimmed and the studio manager introduced the warm-up comedian.

Backstage, Nobby was loving the green room. He had stumbled across it while avoiding the makeup-lady. It had a couple of sofas, a bank of televisions, a drinks tray and plates of sandwiches. He asked a well-dressed man in a sharp-looking suit it was all right if he ate something.

"Yes, yes, I suppose so," the man replied. Nobby quickly demolished a couple of sandwiches and washed them down with a bottle of imported lager.

"Excuse me," he asked of the man. "Did you make these sandwiches? Are they sandwich spread or fish paste? I can't taste things like I used to. See, if they're fish paste then I think I should brush my teeth again because it can't be nice having to interview someone whose breath smells of fish paste."

The man ignored Nobby and turned up the volume on the television, making further conversation difficult.

"It's OK, I think it's sandwich spread," said Nobby.

On the television, a live feed of the warm-up comedian was playing. Nobby wandered over and peered at the screen from behind his sunglasses. The comedian, an American, was wrapping up his act.

"So, there I was in Deptford, trying to get into one of your phone booths. I needed help from a passing stranger to get in because those things are hermetically sealed. Eventually, we managed to pry the door open. It closes, and then that smell hit me. You know what I'm talking about…"

"You ain't kidding," agreed Nobby. He sat down on a sofa and squinted at the televisions. In front of him, the well-dressed man paced nervously, obscuring Nobby's view of the comedian on the screen.

"I bend down to pick up my coins and as I'm coming up for air a see a huge pair of Doc Martins walking towards me. From where I'm looking all I can see are these enormous boots and a head — no body or arms, just 20-hole laces attached to a shaved skull."

The door to the green room opened and an Asian man was ushered in. He bowed and thanked the twentysomething who had escorted him and then turned to Nobby and the well-dressed man. He bowed again.

"Konnichiwa. Good afternoon."

The well-dressed man turned to see who had entered and then turned back to re-check a message on his pager.

Nobby hoisted a bottle of beer in the man's direction as a welcome.

"Cheers. Come on in. Do you want a sandwich? Have you seen this comedian? He's not half-bad."

"Ladies and Gentlemen of the audience, let me ask you a question. If you invented the rotary dialer, what would be the absolute last number you would choose for an emergency call? The number that would be the quickest to dial, right? And what number do you have in this country? Nine. Yes, please take your time going through my wallet. Nine. No problem. kick me again ... Nine!"

Nobby nodded his approval at the television.

"That was funny, all right, but he didn't tell any gags."

Nobby turned to see what the smartly dressed man thought, but a twentysomething with very large headphones and two clipboards had ushered the man out of the room.

"Oh well," said Nobby. "Maybe one more sandwich." He turned to the Asian man who was examining the food.

"Try one."

In the theatre's balcony, Spencer was trying to think of a way he could warn Nobby. The house lights were down as the first guest was interviewed. The balcony was empty so at least Spencer would not be disturbed.

"We need a distraction," Spencer said to himself. "I could faint. No, no one would hear me up here. I could jump!"

Spencer looked down over the balcony rail at the seats far below.

"I could faint very noisily, maybe."

After a while, the house lights went up, the audience clapped politely and the first guest, the smartly dressed man, took a bow and sat back down. Behind Spencer, the door to the balcony opened and a large tour group of Japanese teenagers swarmed through. They quickly, and noisily, took every seat except the one in the far, front corner that Spencer had occupied.

The teenager who sat down next to Spencer smiled and nodded enthusiastically.

"Game show?"

"Excuse me?"

"We are here for the game show," said the teenager in a perfectly articulated English accent. "It's so exciting, isn't it? Have you come far?"

"Wait, no,' said Spencer. "I think you're ... I don't think so. This isn't a game..."

The house lights dimmed again and a voice boomed over the PA system.

"Back in 10, 9, 8, 7, 6 ... Quiet please, ladies and gentlemen." A hush fell over the audience and he light on the studio wall turned red.

"Once again, your host, Helen Hanson!" said the announcer. Helen leaned forward in her chair, scanning the teleprompter.

"Welcome back,' she said. "One more time, we'd like to thank our first guest, the Right Honorable Malcolm Perkins for sparing us a few moments of his time. Later, we will be joined by Akiro Soto, host of Japan's ratings-busting game show, "Dare ga saisho ni sore o kamimashita ka?" which translates as "Who Chewed That First?"

Helen turned to the camera.

"But next, we turn to an item that has caught the public's imagination like nothing else. It was only a couple of days ago that many of us in London and across the country woke up to find a brash new kid on the tabloid block. They eschewed established journalistic standards for a rough and tumble, take-no-prisoners attitude that has made them some enemies on Fleet and Downing Streets, but friends on the High Streets, where their populist, lecturing-free spirit has touched a nerve. Who these publishers are is a complete mystery, except for the grapevine speculation that they draw from many in our homeless population."

Helen paused reading from the teleprompter and spoke directly to the studio audience.

"Honestly, who knew they had that kind of creativity or organization?" she said, flashing one of her legendary smiles before returning to her script.

"Through our many resources we reached out and finally made contact. They agreed send a representative to the show if we kept it a secret. So, please, put your hands together for the Pope of the Pulp, the Down-and-Out Dean of the Diss. Actually, he's so famous right now that he only needs one name. Let's hear it for … Nobby!"

The audience applauded wildly as Nobby poked his head around the curtain. Spencer stood up in the balcony and waved frantically to him, but his efforts were lost as all the Japanese teenagers followed suit — clapping and waving their arms in the mistaken assumption that this was the required response at a game show. Anyway, the tint on Nobby's sunglasses kept him from seeing more than a few feet in front of him.

Helen fetched Nobby from behind the curtain and pulled him onto the stage. She whispered into his ear, off mic.

"Apologies. I don't know who writes all that guff on the prompter. I love what you are doing. Come and sit. We should do lunch sometime. Just you and me."

"Love to!" Nobby replied, basking in the glow of the audience reception.

In the cavern, Kipper, the Editor and many of the others were crowded around the TV set, watching the show. Mavis narrowed her eyes and pursed her lips.

Across town, a projector threw a giant-sized TV picture onto the wall of the Proprietor's office. The Proprietor leaned back in his chair and watched as Helen directed Nobby to his seat."

"Mitchell!" he hissed into a walkie-talkie. "Wait until I give you the word."

Mitchell nodded his head and fiddled with his earpiece.

"So, Nobby," Helen said. "We can deal with questions about The Daily Bread in a minute, but first I'd like to ask you: Why the disguise? What are you trying to hide?"

"My face," Nobby said.

"Well, yes, but why?" asked Helen. "Isn't there a responsibility — if you are writing about people — that the people you are writing about have an opportunity to answer back?"

"I don't know anything about that," Nobby replied. "It's just that some people in this town are out to get us. They've tried to kidnap us and everything. And all we are doing is freedom of the press, giving the people what they want."

"Good lad, Nobby," said the Editor, struggling to hear the interview over the hubbub of background noise in the cavern.

"And you think people want to read these stories backwards?" said Helen.

"Er, yes, that was a strategy of ours…"

"One that seems to have paid off spectacularly well," Helen said enthusiastically.

"Harrumph," snorted the smart-dressed man, now sitting on the far side of the guest couch.

"Ah, Mr. Perkins, you have an opinion on this?" Helen said.

"Yes. It seems to me that our friend here is simply substituting rubbish for refuse. Is there really much of a difference?"

Nobby paused for a second. The smart-dressed man looked familiar, somehow.

"Actually, we're not substituting rubbish; we're recycling it. Recycling is a good thing, ain't it? We go through people's rubbish stories and recycle them."

"Is that where you get most of your leads," asked Helen. "By going through celebrity rubbish?"

"Nobby smiled. "If it's good enough for Scotland Yard ..."

The audience laughed, but back in the cavern the Editor was wary.

"Careful, now," he said to the screen. "We don't need the Old Bill on our backs, too."

Helen waited for the audience to calm down.

"Before we go to break, there may be some people in our audience who haven't read your column. Would you mind reading one of your items? We've cued it up for you."

Spencer could tell that Nobby, even under his disguise, was flustered. Spencer held his breath.

"It's over by camera one," said Helen, pointing in the direction of the teleprompter.

"Er, where, what is it? Nobby stammered.

"Right there," she said. "Under that big camera."

Spencer could barely watch. He stood up, held his breath and got ready to faint as noisily as possible.

"Ah," Nobby said. "I'm sorry dear, but I ain't got my reading glasses. I'm pretty much blind as a bat without 'em."

Spencer exhaled and sat back down.

"Oh well," said Helen. "I suppose our audience will have to wait for your next dispatch. After the break, we'll take questions from our studio audience. Don't go away, we'll be right back."

The studio lights went back up as the show cut away to commercials. Helen leaned over towards Nobby.

"Shrewd move, that ... pretending not to be able to read the prompter! I see what you're doing. Keep them wanting more, so the only place they can read your content is in your column. Ingeniouser and ingeniouser."

"Thanks," said Nobby, comfortable now that the whole teleprompter issue was behind him.

"If I had my way, you'd all be thrown back into whatever cesspool you crawled out of," interjected the smartly dressed man. "It's disgraceful, what you're doing."

"Blimey!" said Nobby as the hammer of recognition thumped down on him. "I know where I've seen you before."

"Well, obviously. I'm a public figure."

"No, mate. You wouldn't be doing this in public." Nobby reached under the waistband of his trousers and pulled out a couple of sheets of paper. He looked at one closely and then waved it around triumphantly.

"See, it is you," he said and showed the page to Helen, who winced when she saw what it contained. Nobby returned the papers to their hiding place and tut-tutted dramatically.

"What the … give me that!" shouted the smartly dressed man. He vaulted across the couch and struggled to grab the papers.

"And we're back," said the announcer.

Returning from the commercial break, television viewers around the country were as shocked as the studio audience to see the Right Honorable Member for North Gravesdon straddling another guest. He held one arm around Nobby's neck; with the other, he attempted to retrieve the incriminating papers. Nobby endeavored to wrestle himself free by extracting the Right Honorable Member's hand from grabbing anything of value — all the while keeping his disguise in place. In between them, Helen Hanson — award-winning journalist and presenter — tried to get them to separate. Only when the studio lights had dimmed and the protagonists realized that they were back live, did they all break and the pandemonium subside.

"Well, you can always count on a lively discussion on this show, right?" said Helen, composing herself. "I think it's best if we take some questions from the audience, don't you? Would everyone please take their seat?"

The studio audience, still cheering and laughing, eventually sat down. The Japanese students were the last to sit as they had whooped it up the loudest. The teenager next to Spencer gave him a smile and a big thumbs-up.

"Brilliant stuff, he said. "Quite brilliant. When do we vote for the winner?"

Below them, Mitchell and his two associates—who had singled out Nobby and had approached the stage—reluctantly returned to their seats.

Helen replaced her lapel mic, dislodged during the fracas.

"OK, who is first?" she said, surveying the audience. "Yes, you sir."

A man stood up in the rear row and a twentysomething rushed over with a wireless mic.

"My question is, if you say you celebrate garbage, how come I've never seen you at Tottenham?"

"Funny, very funny," Helen said. "Anyone with a proper question?"

Thirty or 40 hands shot up and more people stood up. Helen struggled to select someone who she thought might be interesting. Eventually, she settled on a woman at the front.

"Yes, what would you like to say?"

"It doesn't seem right," said the woman.

"What doesn't," Helen asked.

"Him." the woman said, pointing.

The smartly dressed man stood up.

"I can assure you, madam, I had nothing to do with what was in that photograph."

"No, no," she said. "Not you … him." This time there was no mistake. She pointed directly at Nobby.

"Him! It's just that I have two young children and I'm trying to bring them up the right way, the way that their father would have approved of and I when see this gentleman being viewed as someone to be admired, well, it doesn't seem right, that's all. He's no different than the rest of them."

An unruly chorus of boos greeted this party-pooper.

"No, we must let people have their say," Helen said, motioning for the audience to calm down.

Everyone sat down, except a small, middle-aged woman behind Mitchell. She nervously raised a hand.

"Can I say something?"

"Be our guest," Helen replied. The small woman sighed.

"My name is … actually, it doesn't matter what my name is. The point is you ran an article in your column about my husband. You can hide behind all your clever, clever backwards-printing, legal loopholes, but the bottom line is that since your story came out, my son hasn't been able to go to school because of bullying, my daughter had to quit her job and now my husband's pension has been suspended pending an investigation."

Back in his office, the Proprietor leaned forward in his chair.

"Oh my. Thus, doth the pendulum swingeth," he said.

In the studio, the woman wiped her eyes and continued.

"My husband, he's not a public figure — at least, not until now — but he can't go out, even for a drink. Everyone looks at him funny but he's not done anything."

From the rear of the audience a couple of boos were quickly shushed as people strained to hear the woman speak.

"Oh, it's all good clean fun," said Nobby, beginning to wonder if perhaps this had been a mistake.

"Good clean fun? Not for us, it's not! What were you thinking? How could you be so cruel?"

A man stood up at the front.

"Yeah, I was thinking the same thing," he said.

"Sit down," said another man, farther up the aisle. "Most of them need taking down a peg or two. It's a public service, if you ask me."

"Make me," replied the man at the front. Security rushed over to keep the two apart, but disputes were breaking out all through the audience. An elderly woman rolled up a copy of Nobby's column and tried to strike the man standing next to her. Helen attempted to quiet the crowd but it was too late.

"Please, people! Calm down!" Her voice amplified as it was, was lost among all the shouting that pulsed throughout the studio.

Mitchell looked on, baffled at the disagreements that had engulfed the audience. Everyone had risen from their seats; the aisles were blocked with arguing audience members, security and the studio staff who were trying to restore order. Things had taken a nasty turn, and some of the arguments had become physical. Mitchell and his men headed for the stage so Nobby could not escape again.

"Sit down, you idiot!" yelled the Proprietor in his ear. "Let nature take its course." His words went unheeded though, drowned out by the commotion in the studio. The Proprietor pressed the button on his intercom and waited for his secretary to answer.

"Yes, sir,"

"Get me our Editor. I have an idea for a Special Edition. And I think it might be time for me to have another conversation with our monocular friend."

"I'll bring him up, sir."

Back in the studio, Spencer saw his chance to take advantage of all of mayhem. He cupped his hands and yelled as loud as he could.

"Four of clubs! Four of clubs!" Unfortunately, his voice was lost in the brouhaha that rose up from the audience below. Spencer tried again.

"Nobby! Four of clubs!" Still no good. Suddenly, the Japanese student next to him — assuming that this was the required answer to some unrevealed quiz question — began shouting.

"Four of clubs!" he yelled. "Four of clubs!" Soon, the other students followed suit and chanted in unison: "FOUR OF CLUBS! FOUR OF CLUBS!"

The din coming from the balcony cut through the uproar of the arguments radiating from the audience downstairs. It even reached the stage.

Eventually, Nobby noticed something happening up the balcony. He peered over the top of his sunglasses and saw Spencer waving at him. Nobby smiled and waved back, until he realized that Spencer had pointed at someone in the studio audience. He looked over and saw Mitchell and his partners struggling to get to the stage. A mix of brawling audience members, studio security and twentysomething production assistants — headphones askew and microphone cables wrapped around their necks — held them back.

Helen walked to the edge of the stage and pleaded for calm.

"Everyone, please! This is daytime television. There may be children watching!"

Spencer pointed for Nobby to leave the stage and Nobby gave him a thumbs-up.

"Right," Nobby announced to no one. "I'm off!" He shook off the smartly dressed man who had again tried to tackle him in an attempt to retrieve the documents, parted the curtains and made his way back stage.

Once Spencer saw that Nobby had left, he also turned to leave. From out of nowhere, a firm hand grasped his arm and halted his progress up the aisle.

"Hey!" said the Japanese student, his eyes ablaze with excitement. "Best game show *ever*! What do we win?"

Spencer pointed at Mitchell.

"You see those gentlemen down there in the suits? Mr. Mitchell has prizes for all of you."

Spencer dashed up the aisle, down the stairs and out the front door of the studio. He ran down the alleyway and bumped into Nobby, who had exited by the stage door.

"What a palaver that was!" Nobby said. He tossed his sunglasses into a bin and hurried down the alley. "I never should have let him talk me into it."

"What are we going to do?" asked Spencer.

"About what?"

This time, it was Spencer who stopped so suddenly that Nobby tripped over him.

"About what just happened back there! About how you went from Public Spokesman to Public Enemy in about 10 minutes."

"You don't think it will blow over?" asked Nobby.

"You tell me," said Spencer. "Can you think of anyone who might want to take advantage of this?"

Nobby paused. "Right. More than one, probably."

9. HOME TO ROOST

"So, you see," said the Proprietor. "If you really are concerned about them, you'll do the right thing." He sat on the edge of his desk. Next to him was an open bottle of wine and a pair of crystal wine glasses. A large cigar smoldered in an ashtray.

"It's time to make a big decision," he continued. "I'm worried that your associates are out of their depth. It always amazes me how fickle public opinion can be. It likes nothing more than to build people up, only to tear them down the next day."

He refilled one of the glasses, walked back to his side of the desk and sat down.

"So how about it?"

"They're my mates," the visitor said from the comfort of a large armchair. "I would never do anything to hurt them."

"You'd be helping, not hurting them. If you *don't* do anything, that's when the problems could arise."

"I don't know …"

"Caractacus, isn't it?" the Proprietor asked.

Caractacus nodded and took another pull on the cigar. He sat back in his chair and put his feet up on the desk. He folded his arms across his ample belly, resting them on a quilted gilet that he wore over a fine cotton shirt. His old eye patch had gone, replaced with a sharp-looking leather number and an onyx googly-eye now jiggled where the crude line drawing had once observed its surroundings.

"Caractacus was a general, right?" the Proprietor continued. "Generals such as you and me, sometimes we need to make difficult decisions — decisions with which lesser men would struggle. At the end of the day, though, that is how history will judge us — as leaders.

"A general leads from the front," Caractacus said.

"Exactly," agreed the Proprietor. "Take your time, go think about it. By the way, how are the accommodations?"

"Smashing," Caractacus said, rising from his chair. "I would like to stretch my legs though."

"Of course, no problem at all"

The Proprietor put a benevolent arm around Caractacus' shoulder as he guided him out of the office and towards the lift.

"Mitchell here will see you out." He turned to Mitchell who had been waiting outside the office. "Mitchell, would you be so kind?"

Caractacus entered the lift and wandered out of earshot.

"Follow him," the Proprietor whispered to Mitchell.

An hour later, Nobby and Spencer paused outside the door to the cavern.

"I just had a very worrying thought," Nobby said. "If people are angry about what we wrote the first time, how they are going to feel after they read our next one?"

"You mean the column with all that really, really awful stuff that we wrote from the files you found in the cabinet?"

"Don't remind me," moaned Nobby. "We need to scrap it and re-write the whole bloody thing."

"I did try to tell you."

"I know, I know," said Nobby, shaking his head. They pushed the door open and slipped inside.

"Get ready for our normal frosty reaction," Nobby said.

"This time we probably deserve it."

Workers, preparing for the next of edition of The Daily Bread, filled the Cavern. Nobby and Spencer walked down the stairs onto the main floor, but it seemed like no one even noticed them.

"Hey, Shoulders!" Nobby called out. "How's things?"

Shoulders looked up from his desk. He peered at Nobby through his coke-bottle glasses.

"Not bad." he said, quickly returning to his work. Other workers pushed past Nobby and onto their next assignment. Nobby was confused. He had expected anything but this indifference. He walked over to Kipper, who was up to his elbows in grease. He had fitted a very large fan to the back of the printing machine.

"Hey, Kipper. What did you think of me on the telly?"

"Good. Now, pass me those pliers, will you? The needle nose not the bull nose." Nobby meekly handed over the tool, and Kipper retreated around the back of the machine.

"Cooling. She needs more cooling if she's to run at full steam. There, that should do it." Kipper emerged from the rear and wiped his hands on his lapels.

"Now, what were you saying?"

Nobby spoke loudly, making sure that everyone in the cavern could hear him.

"I said, what did you think of me on the telly? You must have seen it?" Finally, the room went quiet.

"Yes, dear, we saw it." Mavis had entered the cavern unnoticed and stood at the top of the stairs.

"I thought it went well, considering," Nobby said.

"I'm not exactly a professional TV critic," she said, "but it seemed to me that you had to run off the stage before the audience tore you to pieces. And that Hanson woman was simply awful. 'Let's do lunch!' You were actually considering it?"

"But it was a Media Event! Think of the publicity, right?"

"Was it ever!" said the Editor, who strode towards Nobby and gave him a hug. "Excellent job! Really raised our profile. We can't wait to read your next column. Let's have it, then."

Nobby turned away and replied with a hint of stuffiness, "It ain't ready."

"Nonsense, the boy has it. You gave it to him before the TV show. Hand it over." The Editor held out his hand.

"I said it ain't ready yet. I need to add some stuff about the show I was just on."

"No time for that. Come on, son. Let's take a gander at it. A deadline is a deadline."

Spencer dug deep into his pocket and pulled out the paper, sighed, and to Nobby's horror and amazement, handed it to the Editor.

"Here you go. Backwards, remember?"

"Wonderful, great. Thanks very much," the Editor said.

Nobby was lost for words. He looked from Spencer to the Editor and then back to Spencer.

"Some friend you are!" He turned around and climbed the stairs to the exit. At the top, Mavis stood in his way. She took Nobby's arm as he tried to leave the cavern.

"Don't be too hasty, dear," she said. "You don't want to do anything you might regret later."

"Yes," agreed the Editor. "Let's see what makes you so unhappy about your latest masterwork."

He gently unfolded the sheet of paper and smoothed it out.

Nobby looked down at Spencer and shook his head in resignation. He turned and faced the crowd that had gathered below and cleared his throat.

"Ahem. Before you do that, there are some things I need to get off my chest. Firstly, what is written in that column, that's not me anymore. It's cruel, probably mostly untrue and — as you all saw on the telly earlier — that stuff is not gonna fly now, anymore." Nobby paused for effect.

"And what's more, I didn't write it."

"Yeah, we know," the Editor said.

"You see, I never learned … wait … what?"

"We know you didn't write it,' continued the Editor. "Red told me that you stole files from the Scribe's office when you rescued Kipper. We have known for a while. So, let's see what kind of filth they've been hiding from all of us, should we?"

"That's not what I meant," said Nobby. "It's not fit to print"

"I'll be the judge of that. If it's not fit to print, then we'll print it to fit, is what I say."

"Nobby!" said Spencer. "Let him read it."

The insistent note in Spencer's voice quieted Nobby's protests. The room grew silent again as the Editor read the column. This time, his lips definitely moved, his eyes narrowed and his brow furrowed.

"No, no, no. This is rubbish," he said.

"Ain't that the idea, boss?" said Shoulders, attempting a joke.

"What is this?" continued the Editor. "Listen …"

At the top of the stairs, Nobby cringed in anticipation, fully aware of the depths to which his column had sunk.

"The Lord Mayor took time out of his busy schedule to attend the annual charity orchid show at the Barbican yesterday. Proceeds benefitted underprivileged children from the East End …"

Nobby — who had clamped both eyes tight shut — opened one and raised an eyebrow. This was not what he had been expecting, at all.

"… the Chancellor of the Exchequer served soup at a homeless shelter on Friday evening …"

"Minestrone," interjected Shoulders. "Needed salt."

Nobby looked at Spencer, who smiled surreptitiously and winked.

"We can't print this!" the Editor exclaimed. "It's not terrible."

"Thank you," Nobby and Spencer said simultaneously.

"No, it's terrible because it's not terrible," exclaimed a frustrated Editor. "It's not about terrible people doing terrible things. It goes on and on about flower shows and benefit dinners and mambo-athons --whatever they are. The only cruel thing about this is how it will bore the readers."

"We don't have a choice," said Kipper. "We print tonight and we've a hole in the paper where Nobby's column should be. He took the paper from the Editor and handed it over for typesetting.

"Let's move it!" he continued. Kipper clapped his hands together in encouragement and returned to work on his press while the other men returned to their chores. Nobby descended the stairs and walked over to Spencer.

"I think you've got some explaining to do," he said quietly.

"Me? What do you mean?"

"You know. How come the stuff I dictated to you mysteriously ended up completely different? Trust is a two-way street, you know."

"Well, yes, but ..."

"So, you took it upon yourself to re-write my column. The column that had taken this town by storm; the column that had made me a rising star; the column that almost got me lynched on live television."

Spencer's jaw dropped.

"You cheeky young beggar!" Nobby whispered in Spencer's ear. "You changed it!"

Spencer grinned. "Apology accepted," he said.

With the ice broken, Nobby picked him up and spun him around.

"I'm sorry," said Spencer. "I couldn't bring myself to write that stuff anymore so I did some of my own research. I was going to tell you but things moved so fast."

"No, it's perfect," Nobby replied. "You saved all of our bacon."

"It's not exactly rocket-science, is it?" said Spencer. "Quite straightforward once you get the hang of it. Re-hash a few press releases, keep your eyes and ears open … pretty soon it almost writes itself. It's actually easier than if you had to make stuff up."

The door to the cavern swung open and Red dashed through.

"Everyone, take a look at this!" Red waved a newspaper over his head as he leapt down the stairs, two at a time and handed it to the Editor.

It was a copy of The Scribe, headlined, "Special Edition: The Dosser Dossiers." The main photograph was of Nobby on the Helen Hanson Show attempting to fend off the smartly-dressed man who was draped all over him in a seemingly compromising position. The accompanying story frequently used such words as "shocking" and "expose" while also referring to "The Vile Files."

The Editor flicked through some of the other pages. On Page 3, a photograph was captioned 'pretty vagrant" — a scantily clad young woman whose makeup had been deliberately smudged and whose clothes seemed to consist of strips of duct tape and torn shopping bags.

"What does it say?" asked Nobby.

"Well, you've seen the front page," replied the Editor. "But there's also a story from their political correspondent on Page 4. It says here that says you have spent a lot of time in the Soviet Union." The Editor began to read from the article.

"Comrade Nobbyski's KGB Cutie Uncovered! Unnamed sources confirm that recent media darling and erstwhile newspaper columnist spent many of his formative years in Mother Russia, although much of his time was spent in the company of a much younger — and more attractive — female operative who we can reveal was later recruited by the KGB."

"What? That's nonsense!" said Nobby. "I mean blimey, I was in the Navy for years and we visited Russian ports now and then, but that's just false. They're making this stuff up!"

"I told you he was a Red!" said Red, excitedly. "Giving the paper away for free, indeed!"

The Editor leafed through more pages.

"The remainder seems to be a hundred-percent clone of our first edition," he continued. "The real kick-in-the teeth, though, is this '*Spot the Bum*' competition. There's a five-grand prize for anyone who can find our location."

"Five grand?" said Odds-On. "That's a lot, that is."

Nobby, if we're going to compete, I'll need those files you took," the Editor said.

"No, no," said Nobby. If they go low, we should go high."

Spencer chimed in.

"That's right! Differentiation! My father was always talking about that."

The Editor peered over the top of the newspaper at them.

"This ain't no broadsheet," he said. "We don't do high. Give me those files."

"No!" Nobby said. "This has already gone far enough."

"Give me those files!"

Red tapped the Editor on the shoulder.

"We don't need them, Boss," he said. "I have my own that I took from the cabinets."

With a flourish, Red produced a number of manila folders and handed them over to the Editor. The Editor leafed through them briefly.

"Oh, this is good stuff," he leered. "Hold the presses!"

***

Later that night, a group of men trooped up another long flight of stairs to deliver the next edition. Nobby had spent the whole evening trying to convince the Editor to take the high ground. The Editor however, was having none of it.

"Write what you know, and we know all about muck," he had insisted in the Cavern as The Daily Bread was going to print.

"You're not changing my column," Nobby said.

"I wouldn't dream of it," replied the Editor. "Besides, we have plenty of content that will balance out your sanctimonious scribblings."

"Make your mind up," said Nobby. "Do you like it or not?"

"He doesn't," said Spencer. "He was being rude."

The Editor turned to face Spencer.

"And what exactly is your function here now, eh? Aside from being the designated sidekick, that is. I would think now would be the time to move on to a more wholesome activity for a kid your age."

Nobby jumped in to defend Spencer.

"Don't you talk to him like that!"

"Really?" continued the Editor. "You think you know what's going on here, son? You don't know anything. I know more than you'll ever know."

"I'm not sure I understand," said Spencer.

The Editor hitched a thumb at Nobby. "I know he's not your friend, for one thing."

"Yes, he is. Why would you say that?"

Nobby put a protective arm around Spencer.

"Come on, I think this might be a good time to leave," he said. The pair walked up the stairs to the door of the Cavern.

The Editor followed them up the stairs. He continued to jab an accusatory figure at Nobby.

"You really think it was a coincidence that you found him in your shed? It happens all the time, right? Strange men camped out in garden sheds making friends with kids who have a parent employed in a line of work about which we know nothing? You think that was serendipity at work? Happenstance? Afraid not. Your friend here had been camped out there for days before you wandered in."

"No, that's not true," said Spencer. He looked over at Nobby.

"OK," said the Editor. "Let's go with that. He was supposed to be there in the morning, right? Only he wasn't because he had to report back to me that he had made contact with the son and heir."

"That's enough," Nobby said.

"Wake up and smell the coffee, kid. That whole performance when you first walked in here … that was staged. He told me he was bringing you in."

"I didn't' know," said Kipper from atop his press.

"I didn't know, either," agreed Red.

"No one knew, apart from Nobby and me," continued the Editor. "We had to find a way to get to someone who knew about distributing a newspaper. Those blokes never go out drinking or carousing after work so we couldn't get to them to learn their trade. Nobby comes up with this plan to get someone to do the questioning for us, and then we would get the information from them."

"Is it true?" Spencer looked at Nobby.

"Now, wait," Nobby said. "I can explain. I thought we talked about this."

"Go ahead," encouraged the Editor. Nobby looked down and

shuffled his feet.

"Well …"

Spencer opened the door. "That's OK," he said. He slipped through and slammed it shut behind him. The echo reverberated around the cavern.

For a few seconds there was silence in the room.

"OK people, back to work!" said the Editor, clapping his hands in encouragement. "Kipper, fire up that thing and give it the full beans this time. We're behind schedule!"

"I don't know about beans," said Kipper, "But I can get her running at about two-thirds full power. That should be plenty."

Kipper started the press. He turned the key and pressed the button. The large fan that he had added began to rotate. The room shook as the machine gathered speed. The noise was so loud that although Kipper saw Nobby talking to Mavis, he had no idea what he was saying to her. All he knew was that sometime between the printing of The Daily Bread and their second ascent up seemingly endless flights of stairs to deliver it, both Nobby and Mavis had vanished.

***

"This doesn't feel right, doing this without Nobby." Kipper complained to the Editor, as he carried both his and Nobby's bundles of newspapers up the stairs.

"Please," replied the Editor. "He'll get over it. Give him a day or two and he will be right as rain. He knows what side his bread is buttered."

"So far it always seems to fall butter-side down," grumbled Odds-On.

The men reached to top floor and looked around. This time, there was no sense of achievement or wonder, simply a group of men carting large canvas bags to the top of an empty building.

"Where is this place?" asked Red.

"Aye, you never tell us," agreed Kipper. "We just appear out of the Tube line, into a basement and up the stairs."

"Centrepoint," replied the Editor. "Obviously, we couldn't go back to the GPO Tower, but this is the next best thing. It's centrally located — no lights at night and all these upper floors have been empty for years."

"It's flippin' freezin' up here!" complained Red. "Can't we just chuck them out now and be done with it?"

"Of course not. Morning rush hour is the only time. We just need to settle down for the night and we'll be done first thing in the morning."

***

After leaving the Cavern, Spencer made his way back home. As he opened the back door, he took one last wistful look in the direction of the shed.

Inside his house, his mother was asleep on the couch, snoring lightly. He padded upstairs and examined the marks on his bedroom door where it had been forced open by the heavies. He turned on his TV but could not find anything worth watching. Soon, he too drifted off to sleep.

He awoke with a start. He could not have been out for long because the same show was still on the TV. Approaching form down the street, he heard a few Christmas carolers break into a ragged chorus.

"Goodness, they're awful," Spencer thought. The singing soon stopped, replaced by an instrumental version of Jingle Bells. There was no mistaking this particular version.

Spencer leapt off his bed and just as quickly leapt back on it. He was annoyed with himself; after all, hadn't they lied to him from the beginning? The music became louder as the carolers approached. Spencer didn't know what to do. He stood up, and then sat back down again. He paced around his room, biting his fingernails.

Then, right outside his house, the music stopped. Spencer held his breath, waiting to see what would happen next. Nothing happened next, nothing except the wind moving through the trees. He took an angular peek out of his window, not wanting anyone to see him looking. Spencer sat on his bed just as the first pebble cracked against his bedroom window.

"Go away," Spencer half whispered, half-yelled. A second pebble soon followed.

"Nobby! Go away!"

"It's not Nobby," whispered a woman's voice from outside.

Spencer ran to the window and opened it. In the darkness, he saw a familiar figure.

"Mavis?"

"That's right, dear."

"What are you doing here?"

"Nobby asked me to come."

"Where is he?" Spencer peered into the darkness, but Mavis was alone.

"He's embarrassed."

"Yeah, well, so would I if I'd spent all that time lying to a child."

"Don't be too hard on him. He really is very fond of you."

"I thought you were my friend."

"Oh, Spencer, we are your friends," Mavis implored. "Things just happened so quickly. It all got out of control. We're so sorry."

Out of the darkness, Spencer heard Nobby's muffled voice call out from inside the shed.

"I never lied to you."

"Excuse me?" said Spencer. The door to the shed swung open and Nobby ambled out.

"I never lied to you," he repeated. "You've every right to be angry at me, but I want you to know that. I never lied to you."

"So, tell me the truth now. How many days were you in the shed before I walked in?"

"Just a few, I think."

Spencer raised his voice. "How many?"

"Three."

"Wow, three whole days."

"We were desperate," Mavis said. "We were almost ready to print but, as you know, we had no idea about that side of things."

"You knew, too?" Spencer asked Mavis.

"No, no, I didn't know until Nobby told me today."

"OK, good."

"Although, if I'm being really truthful, I would probably have gone along with it."

Nobby reached out and took Mavis's hand. Mavis smiled at him.

"But then we got to know you," said Nobby. "And you were a really great kid — so kind and thoughtful — and we did so many great things together."

"Yeah, throwing those papers out the Tower was pretty cool," Spencer said.

"Don't forget the show on the telly," said Nobby. "How many

people do you know who almost got beaten up on live TV? And it was you who got me out of there in one piece."

"I did do that," Spencer said.

"As I said, you have every right to be angry. I want you to know, though, as we got to know you, it became harder and harder to tell you everything about how we met. There just never seemed to be the right moment."

"You should have tried, at least."

"Again, correct." Nobby paused for a second. "Spencer, do you still have that penny whistle I gave you?"

"Yeah."

Nobby walked back over to the shed.

"I'm going to spend a little more time in here. When you're ready to talk more, give it a toot and I'll come out."

"Maybe I will, maybe I won't" said Spencer.

"Your choice. I don't want to think of you being angry with me for any longer than is necessary, so I'll be here until we can work something out."

Spencer was a little perplexed. He watched Nobby enter the shed and close the door behind him. Now it was just him and Mavis.

"This has been hard on him too, you know," she said. "The newspaper, how we were all going to find somewhere nice to live … that was all he ever talked about. Now it looks like it's over, almost before it began."

"I'm sorry," Spencer said. "I'm sorry that it didn't turn out like it was planned."

"That's OK, dear. "We have dealt with all sorts of disappointments through the years. We'll get by."

Spencer leaned on the windowsill with his elbows and rested his chin in his hands.

"Mavis, can Nobby read or write?"

"No, dear, he cannot," she whispered. "I tried to teach him a couple of times but he didn't have the patience for it."

"So, you knew I was helping him?"

"He didn't tell me directly, but I figured it out."

Spencer thought about this.

"Maybe I could teach him."

"I'm sure he'd love that. He values your opinion greatly, you know."

"OK, I'll think about it," Spencer said with a yawn. "I'm going to turn in now."

"Probably a good idea," Mavis said. "I think I'll do the same. Goodnight."

Spencer closed the window and went back to bed. He took one last peak out at the shed and then pulled the covers over his head.

10. PRESS GANGED

It was still dark when the Editor noticed that Kipper was awake, fiddling with the dial on his transistor radio, adjusting an earphone and then re-tuning his radio. The Editor squatted down next to him.

"What's the matter? Can't sleep?"

"That's right, I bought my radio with me in case I got bored and now I'm hearing on it that there are some bad people out there tonight."

"How so?"

"Random acts of violence and stuff. Not many details yet, but it's down on the Street."

"Animals," said the Editor. "We're better off up here, out of the way."

"Aye, said Kipper. "That, we are."

Spencer was also awake early. He tossed and turned as the events of the past few days played through his mind. Eventually, he gave up trying to sleep and sat up. The television was still on and the reflection of the black and white picture flickered across the walls of his bedroom. Spencer tried not to look out of his window at the shed, so he concentrated on the pictures on the TV.

What he saw shocked him. He turned up the volume to hear what the reporter was saying.

"Overnight, we have received numerous reports of roving bands of youths bent on intimidating many of the city's homeless in an attempt to claim the five thousand-pound bounty offered by The Scribe. These efforts reached their nadir when a group of homeless men were seriously assaulted on Bouverie Street."

The camera cut to a shot of the narrow street that led from Fleet Street to the Embankment. Slowly, it panned over to a group of old men interviewed by a reporter. Spencer moved even closer to the television, his face almost pressed against the screen.

"We never stood a chance," said one of the old men. "They were on us like a pack of dogs, they were. All they would say was, *'We want our five grand.. Give us our money. Where's yer newspaper, you old git?'* Stuff like that. We tried to make it to St. Bride's but it was useless. They beat us with sticks, and Jakey was in real bad shape; they nearly killed him, they did. And we don't know nothing."

"And even if we did know where it was, we wouldn't tell," chimed in another man to the rear of the group.

Even though the eyepatch had changed, Spencer recognized Caractacus immediately. His googly eye wobbled erratically as he paced up and down, talking to himself and shaking his head. His face was bruised and his one good eye looked like it was closing.

Caractacus pushed his way through the other men and shouted straight into the camera.

"Mark my words. If someone doesn't do something now, people are going to get hurt! A lot of people! Someone has to take the lead!"

Spencer ran over to the window, opened it and hissed at the shed.

"Nobby!" There was no response. He tried again, but still nothing stirred.

He ran back to his desk and rummaged through the contents until he found the penny whistle. He blew on it tunelessly, like a constable calling for assistance. Finally, he hurled it at the shed, where it hit and cracked a windowpane.

"Nobby! Get up!" After a few seconds there was some stirring— then crashing--from within the shed. Nobby had reacquainted himself with Spencer's skateboard, the paint cans, the old lawnmower and finally the door. He tumbled out onto the crazy paving, still half-asleep.

"OK, jump!" he said. "I'll catch you!"

"I don't need to jump," said Spencer. "But we do need to go … right now!"

***

On the top floor of Centerpoint, Kipper had come to the same conclusion.

"But I have to go!" he pleaded with the Editor. "Can't you understand what's happening?

"Yes, we have to deliver this paper when it gets light."

"Are you daft, man?" Kipper was incredulous. "We canna wait 'til then. I have to get back to the cavern."

"What for? It ain't going anywhere."

"Listen to what I've been telling you!" Kipper waved his radio at the Editor. "People have been hurt. Our people! Now there are all sorts roaming the streets trying to find us. If someone talks, they could lead them right back to the Cavern. Nobby could be there. Mavis could be there. And worse!"

Kipper suddenly got a faraway look in his eyes as he thought about what a bunch of vandals might do to his beloved printing press.

"Nobby can look after himself," the Editor said. "Anyway, he should be here with us, not sulking like a teenager."

Kipper squared up to the Editor, his eyes suddenly blazing.

"Nobby's my friend," he said. "He would have been here if you had done what he asked. And you're right, he can look after himself, but there's someone back there who cannot."

Kipper tossed his bundle of newspapers at the Editor who caught them and staggered backwards under their weight.

"Here," Kipper said, "do your own dirty work. We should never have listened to you!"

In the dim, pre-dawn shadows, it was hard to separate the men from the sacks of newspapers where they slept. Kipper stumbled over a number of the bundles. Some were men and some were newspapers. One was Red. "Is it time?" he asked, rubbing his eyes.

"Aye, time for me to leave," Kipper said. He bounded down to the ground floor, slipped through the security door and onto Oxford Street. Kipper paused to catch his breath, bending over with his hands resting on his knees. A group of young men approached.

"Oy, you," shouted their leader, a stringy youth with a lopsided haircut. "Yes, you, you filthy wino. Where you hiding it, eh?"

Kipper, still hunched over, was trying to regain his breath.

"I'm sorry, my friend. I don't know what you're talking about. You must have me confused with someone else. I don't drink."

"And I'm the Lord Mayor of London," the youth said. "Tell us where the flippin' paper is, otherwise someone might get damaged."

"I'd hate to see anyone get hurt, so, I'll tell you where the paper is." Kipper slowly pulled himself up to his full height until his massive frame towered over his assailants-to-be.

The gang took a few steps back. They had not been expecting resistance and their mob courage evaporated when confronted by this huge, wild-eyed behemoth in front of them.

"Take a wee peek up there," said Kipper, pointing upwards.

Newspapers had begun to float to the ground. Wind-swept and whirling, they seemed to taunt the gang, whose members tried to grab a handful that always seemed to be just out of reach.

"Go home boys. Your mothers will be wondering where you are," said Kipper, walking towards the group.

Adolescent aggression was now in full retreat in the face of an adversary who could fight back.

"Yeah, well, we don't need you, anyways," said the haircut, backing down the street. "We'll find someone who knows what we want."

"And if you do, then I'll find you, and believe me, it will be ugly. Now, get out of my way!"

Kipper feigned a few threatening paces towards the gang, who turned tail and bolted. Kipper shook his fist — more for effect than for any real threat — then hurried for the nearest Tube station entrance.

Kipper navigated through numerous corridors in the Tube system until he was outside the door leading to the cavern. He pulled out a key, but realized the door was already unlocked. The protective metal gate swung open; Kipper pushed the door inward and entered cautiously.

"No, no, no; this isn't good at all," he said, closing the door behind him. The weak glow of a light bulb that flickered and buzzed in its failing health, illuminated the room

"We never leave the light on," Kipper whispered to himself. He walked to the far end of the room and climbed down the ladder into the room with all the pipes.

This room had almost no light, but he knew it so well that he bypassed all the pipes and tubes until he came to the door with 'DAGNER,'— written in Nobby's childlike scrawl — that marked the entrance to the cavern. Kipper tried to push the door open but it would not budge. He put all his weight behind it but it wouldn't budge; something had to be blocking it on the other side. Kipper put his ear to the door and listened. The noise he heard was both immediately familiar and intensely worrying.

"Oh, no!" he wailed, no longer worried if anyone heard him.

"Who's in there?" he shouted at the door. "Let me in! Nobby is that you?"

"No. I'm right here," came a voice out of the darkness.

"Who's that?" Kipper said. "Come out where I can see you."

Spencer and Nobby emerged. "Boy are we glad to see you," Nobby said. "What with everything that's been going on we was worried about you."

"Aye," said Kipper. "I witnessed some of it myself. There's all sorts looking to cause trouble out there."

"Who is in there?" asked Nobby, pointing to the door.

"I don't know," said Kipper, "But whoever it is, they've started my press. I'd know that sound anywhere."

Kipper walked back to the door and started banging on it.

"Hey! Let us in! You canna be running my machine like that!"

Still no response from inside the Cavern.

"Spencer said he saw some of our boys on the news," said Nobby. "They were in trouble."

"Aye, I heard it on the radio," said Kipper. "Those low-lives have stirred up a hornets' nest with that reward offer. Five thousand is a handsome amount of money."

"Do you think it's outsiders in there?" Spencer asked. "What are they doing?"

"If they'd open the door, I could find out!" replied Kipper. He thumped on the door again.

The noise from the press grew louder. Someone had increased its speed. Kipper laid his hand on the door. Now he could feel the vibration from the machine pulsating through the door itself. Kipper was getting increasingly desperate.

"Please. Turn it down!" he screamed through the door. "She's not ready!"

"Kipper?" replied a muffled voice from the other side of the door. "Is that you?"

Kipper — who had slumped disconsolately to the foot of the door — quickly jumped back to his feet.

"Carrot?" Nobby said. "Where have you been? You've been gone for ages."

"It ain't Carrot!" shouted Caractacus from inside. "It's Caractacus."

"OK, OK. Let us in." Kipper said. There was no response.

"Caractacus. Let us in!" Kipper repeated.

"I'm sorry. I can't do that," he said.

"What did you say?" Kipper said as the din from the press made discussion difficult through the door.

"I'm not opening the door," said Caractacus.

Then he volunteered, "I didn't tell them nothing. I could have told them everything, but I didn't tell them nothing. They wanted to follow me here, but it's OK, I lost them."

"That's great," Nobby said.

"They put me up in a posh room, gave me the best grub. Really looked after me. Do you know what a cheroot is? I do."

"Who gave you these things?" asked Nobby. "What did they want?"

"I bet it was The Scribe," Spencer said. The noise kept increasing as the press gathered speed, making it almost impossible to hear.

"They said you were out of your depth," Caractacus shouted over the din. "They said that people might lose their jobs, that someone was going to get hurt if you continued. They were right too — look what's happened."

"But they are the ones doing the hurting!" Nobby yelled.

"Just let us in and we can talk like reasonable folk," said Kipper. Caractacus was not listening.

"I wasn't going to tell them anything, but I couldn't put any more people in danger," he said. "A general has to make tough decisions, even if they are unpopular. I can't let this go on any longer. It's only going to get worse."

"What are you talking about?" shouted Kipper. "Don't do anything foolish."

"Caractacus! You're right," Nobby said. "We made a pig's ear of most of this, but let's talk about how to fix it."

"Fix it? You can't fix this. There are people on all sides who don't want it fixed. What they want is mayhem, they want chaos! And who knows more about chaos …"

Caractacus' voice drifted off as he moved away from the door.

He walked to the printing press and climbed the ladder to the platform of the machine. He pulled hard on a gear lever and the machine shook in response. The fan that Kipper had attached to the press now ran at full speed. Rivets began to pop and the entire mechanism twisted its way loose from its moorings. Caractacus had to grip the railing to stop being hurled onto the floor below. The whole room shook under the force of the machine that now glowed red-hot. Metal on metal shrieked in torture.

Behind the door, pipes began to rattle and shake, dislodging clouds of dust that billowed into the air. Spencer and Nobby backed away, but Kipper continued to bang on the door fruitlessly.

"No, turn it off! Please!"

Caractacus' one good eye blazed. His knuckles gripped the railing of the press as the Cavern began to crumble around him.

"I'm sorry, everyone!" he shouted amid the din.

The noise was deafening. Ancient brickwork disintegrated as the vibration loosened the mortar and powerful spurts of water began to shoot through the gaps. Lights hanging from the ceiling rocked, and the massive fan blew spare copies of the Daily Bread into a maelstrom of dust and dirt. Suddenly, the wall behind the press gave way to the pressure of the water and it crashed down onto the floor. Thousands of gallons of Thames water rushed into the Cavern. As the cold water hit the hot press, the machine ruptured in a catastrophic, twisted-metal-and-steam-driven explosion. Caractacus was thrown from the machine and landed astride a roll of newsprint that had been ejected from the press. He disappeared down the rail tunnel, carried away on a tidal wave of river water and office-equipment flotsam, whooping like a crazed rodeo cowboy riding a diabolical, cylindrical steer, his onyx googly eye convulsing wildly.

Outside the Cavern, Spencer watched as a small puddle leaked into the room from under the door. The noise from the other side of the door slowly subsided until a slight hiss of steam was all that remained. No one said anything. Kipper wiped his eyes. Spencer glanced at Nobby for some direction and Nobby silently put a finger to his lips. Eventually, Kipper wiped his nose with the back of a filthy sleeve and sighed.

"There's not much point in hanging around here," he said, heading back to the ladder.

"But don't you want to see what happened in there?" Spencer

asked.

"I know what happened," Kipper replied. "And it's the last thing I want to see."

Spencer and Nobby followed Kipper up the ladder up to the utility room. Neither cared about the aroma anymore. When they reached the maintenance room, they found Kipper crouched down, leaning against the outside door with his head in his hands.

"Come on, mate," said Nobby, resting a hand on his friend's shoulder. "It's OK. We'll get through this."

Now it was Kipper's turn to put a finger to his lips.

"Don't be daft, man," he whispered. "Shhh. There's someone outside. I think they're coming in."

Kipper pressed his ear against the door. Nobby and Spencer moved behind a maintenance cabinet. After a few seconds, the door creaked open. Kipper flipped the light switch off and ducked behind the cabinet.

"Psst. Is anyone there?" the newcomer asked. Spencer recognized the voice and was about to stand up when Nobby squeezed his arm.

"OK, coast is clear," continued the voice. "Let's go. There's a ladder at the far end." Two men clambered over the equipment towards the ladder. Then Kipper flipped the light switch.

"Well, well, well, what do we have here?" he said.

Odds-On and Mitchell spun around. Nobby and Spencer stood up alongside Kipper.

"Ah. Hello, boys. Er, let me explain," Odds-On stammered.

"Not necessary," Nobby said.

"So, this is how it is?" said Kipper.

"Wait! It's complicated."

"You don't need to explain yourself to these has-beens," Mitchell said, his voice dripping with contempt.

"Better than a never-was," Nobby retorted.

"Aye," added Kipper. "Playing both sides as always, eh Odds-On?"

"It's called a 'Reversed Forecast' said Odd-On, defensively. "And five grand is a *lot* of money."

"Good luck collecting it," Nobby said.

Someone else tapped gently on the door with a cane.

"Excuse me, gentlemen," the Proprietor said. "May I come in?"

Instinctively, everyone took a step back.

"So, this is it, is it?" he continued, looking around the machine room. "Not exactly what I pictured." He brushed some dust off his lapels, and put a small handkerchief to his nose.

"No sir," said Mitchell. "Apparently, this is only the entryway. The main location is a couple of levels below."

"I see," mused the Proprietor. "I can't see myself going down there. These really are the deepest, darkest, dirtiest depths of the city, aren't they?"

Spencer could hold back no longer. "Well, you should know!" he shouted. The Proprietor spun around to face him and Spencer quickly retreated into the folds of Nobby's greatcoat.

"Ah. Finally. I get to meet the brains of the operation." The Proprietor doffed an imaginary cap to Spencer and then Nobby.

"Bravo. I must say, you've led us on quite a merry dance over these last few days. A goose-chase, a bootless-errand, a treasure hunt … and for my own treasure, no less."

"Sorry to tell you, you're too late, mate" said Nobby. "It's over."

"Far from it, my friend," replied the Proprietor. "Your trifling endeavors have reinvigorated the sector, just when we needed it the most, prior to our relocation. In fact, our last issue — in which you figured so prominently — was our most popular ever. For that, I must congratulate you."

"You're not welcome," huffed Nobby.

The Proprietor smiled benignly and turned to Mitchell.

"Mitchell, would you escort these gentlemen from these premises? We'll take over from here, thank you."

"Don't bother," said Kipper. "We can find our own way out. It's all yours."

A fleeting look of puzzlement flickered from the Proprietor's eyes as he contemplated why he was being given the keys to the kingdom so easily. However, the moment quickly passed and he stepped aside to let Nobby, Kipper and Spencer through.

"Good day, gentlemen."

The threesome exited quietly through the gate, past a pair of tight-suited heavies who now flanked the door and back out into the Tube corridor. Suddenly, there was a good deal of noise coming from the other direction. Running towards them down the corridor were Red, the Editor and many of the other men who had spent the night on the top floor of Centerpoint. They slowed down as they approached.

"What's happened?" the Editor asked breathlessly.

"Och, it's over," Kipper said.

"There's no need to rush," said Nobby. "Take as much time as you want."

Red stared at the metal door, his jaw jutting in the direction of the Proprietor and the heavies.

"What are they doing here?" he asked.

"It doesn't matter," replied Nobby. "They're too late, also. They just don't know it yet."

The two groups passed each other warily, one group heading for the Cavern, the other out to the exit.

Mavis was outside, and almost ran into Nobby.

"Oh, Nobby, are you OK? I was so worried."

"I'm fine dear, don't worry about me," he said.

Nobby took one last look back at the door. The Editor had gently tapped the Proprietor on the shoulder and was holding out his hand, perhaps introducing himself.

"Mavis!" hissed Nobby. "What are they talking about?"

Mavis stopped and turned to look back. She squinted into the distance and studied the Editor's lips.

"He's asking for a job."

"Unbelievable!" said Nobby, shaking his head.

"You knew Mavis could read lips?" Spencer said. "I thought it was a secret?"

"So did I," Mavis said.

"I may not be able to read, but I ain't stupid,' Nobby said.

"You can't read?" Kipper said with surprise.

Nobby sighed. "Long story."

***

Nobby, Spencer, Mavis and Kipper wandered aimlessly through the Underground corridors until they reached an exit. Spencer blinked as the harsh morning sunlight struck his face. The streets were full of early commuters, but the threesome was quiet, oblivious to the hustle. Nobby broke the silence.

"That's it then, I suppose," said Nobby.

"Aye, it looks like it," agreed Kipper. Spencer frowned, annoyed by the resignation in their voices.

"You're giving up?"

"What option do we have?"

"I don't know."

"Let's face it, kid. It's over," Nobby said. "And you know what, all things considered, it's probably for the best."

"So now what?" Spencer asked.

"We'll go back to doing what we've always done." Nobby replied. "Getting by."

They wandered into a park where the drone of traffic and the throng of commuters had waned.

Kipper pointed over to a couple of park benches where two homeless men slept. Copies of the Daily Bread had floated down and covered them. They found another bench and sat down.

Spencer turned to Kipper. "What are you going to do?"

"Don't mind me. I'll find something. Somewhere in the country, perhaps. I've always fancied doing up an abandoned water mill. I could rig up all kinds of contraptions and enjoy the scenery for a while."

Now it was Nobby's turn. Spencer was almost too afraid to ask.

"And you?"

Nobby turned to Mavis and smiled.

"I think we'll just lay low for a while. Mavis has a fashion gig in Eastbourne and has been nagging me to go with her. Perhaps this time I should."

Mavis squeezed his hand.

"Wow, that's great," Spencer said.

"Will you be OK?" Mavis asked Spencer.

"Me? I'll be fine."

Kipper stood up to leave. Spencer paused for a second and made a decision. He ran over and hugged Kipper, even though it meant his eyes burned and the back of his throat stung.

"See you around?" he said.

"Aye, most likely."

The four of them stood around quietly.

"I think I should be going," Spencer said. "Mum has to be missing me by now."

"Of course, she is," Nobby said. "She's your mum ain't she?"

"Bye, then."

"I believe they say, 'Au Revoir,' in Eastbourne."

Spencer headed for the park gates. Nobby, Mavis and Kipper waved goodbye. Spencer smiled and waved back. He reached the gates and — having finally sorted out what he wanted to say — turned back around, but they had gone.

***

Spencer stalled returning to his home and its grey normalcy. He meandered through some of the larger toy shops but his heart was not in it. Unable to put it off any longer, he found himself at his house. He headed for the back door, pausing to glance over at the shed. The door was cracked open and a flashlight twinkled through the broken window.

Spencer's eyes opened wide with amazement. He dashed down the path and threw open the door.

"You're back here, already?" he yelled with delight.

"That's right, son, I am," said his father from the far end of the shed. Harry, wrapped in his grimy gabardine, was trying to keep warm. In one hand, he held the flashlight and in the other a newspaper that lay open at the jobs page.

"Your mother won't let me back in the house. Could you put in a good word for me?"

"OK. Yeah, of course," Spencer said, trying to hide his disappointment. He peered behind his father, eventually resigning himself to the fact that there was no one else in the shed.

"That's a good boy. And, if you get the chance, could you bring me a meat pie? There should still be one left in the fridge. If not, then how about a sandwich? Fish paste would be splendid."

"Sure," said Spencer, navigating his exit.

"Oh, Spencer," Harry said. "Once more thing."

Spencer stopped at the door and turned around.

"Can I ask how the newspaper publishing business is going?"

Spencer thought long and hard before answering.

"Disappointing," he said. "Probably the best way to describe it."

"Yes," Harry said. "It often is."

Father and son stared into the distance. Eventually, Harry broke the silence.

"Oh well, no use crying over spilled milk and all that. Actually, a glass of milk with the sandwich would be great too. Or the meat pie, whatever works for you is fine with me."

Harry's voice tailed off as Spencer left the shed. He dragged himself through the back door.

"Spencer, there you are!" his mother said. She carried a wine glass in each hand and her heels clicked on the linoleum as she moved from the kitchen, through the hall and into their front room.

"Come in here," she said. "I want you to meet someone." Spencer reluctantly followed her.

"Spencer, I want you to meet Morris. Morris works at the Tribute. In case you were wondering, that's his company car outside."

A middle-aged man in a cheap suit stood up and held out his hand for Spencer to shake. Spencer examined the hand, with its bitten nails and swollen fingers. The wristwatch was nice though.

"Nice to meet you, son," said the man. Spencer smiled, shook the man's hand and turned to his mother.

"Can I go now?" he asked.

"Yes, run along. Dinner is in the microwave."

Spencer climbed the stairs to his room. He spent the next few hours changing the channels on his TV searching for stories about the newspaper, the cavern flooding, or the beatings some of the homeless had endured the previous night. Daytime television was light on hard news, though, so Spencer settled for a rerun of the Helen Hanson Show.

A couple of hours later, he was awakened by a pebble tossed against the glass of his bedroom window.

"Dad! OK, I'm sorry. I forgot," he said, opening the window. "Fish paste sandwich, right?

"A sandwich would be lovely," Nobby said from below, "But right now we have more important fish to fry."

Spencer clamped his own hand over his mouth to stop himself from crying out until he could compose himself.

"What are you doing here?"

"Come on down and I'll tell you," Nobby said. "And take the stairs… no jumping."

Spencer tiptoed down the stairs and out the back door. He ran over to Nobby and gave him a hug.

"Listen," Nobby said. "I've got something to tell you."

"Not here," Spencer said, pointing to the shed. "My dad is in there."

"Lucky man," Nobby replied. "OK then, come on." Nobby took Spencer by the hand and they walked along the side path and out onto the street.

"What is it?" Spencer asked.

"Well, after you left, Kipper and I visited some of our old haunts," said Nobby. "We wanted to make sure that everyone was all right, what with all that trouble the night before. We got talking to some blokes we hadn't seen for a while. One of them said that they had heard a rumor about a TV studio on the north side of town that was closing down. Elstree, I think they said. Apparently, the BBC is looking to take it over, but they don't want any of the old equipment."

Spencer stopped dead in his tracks, making Nobby accidentally barge into him from behind.

"No!"

"Yeah, they just dumped it all on the side of the street! Kipper is up there now. We can take anything we want, and we don't even have to steal it!"

"Kipper can fix it all?"

"Please. And some of it isn't even broken, just old"

"What do we know about television?"

"A good deal more than we thought we knew about newspapers. Don't forget we have previous experience."

"I'm not sure that counts," said Spencer. "We caused a riot and had to run out of there."

"That made good TV, though, right?"

"That's true. The kid next to me told me he thought it was the best game show he'd ever seen."

"Game show?"

"I know. He was confused."

They walked towards the subway station as a street light flickered and turned on.

"What would I do there?" Spencer said.

"Help put the team back together, for one thing."

"And you?"

"Any job where I don't have to read, obviously."

"I could teach you."

"That you could," said Nobby. "It's about time I learned, ain't it?"

"Probably," Spencer agreed.

"How about a weatherman? I could be a weatherman," Nobby said. "Do they need to read? I know the weather better than most people."

"I think they need to read the weather reports."

"Right," said Nobby. "Sports. I like sports. I could be the boxing correspondent."

"You know, with all your Navy experience I think you might make a good ..." Spencer paused for effect. "A good anchor."

"Funny. Very funny." Nobby feigned a few punches at Spencer, who dodged them easily as they rounded the corner.

***

Street tile, corner of Fleet Street and St. Dunstan's Court,
London EC4.
The inscription reads…

*"1980's new computer printing technology brought about the demise of the
traditional Fleet Street printing process."*

ABOUT THE AUTHOR

Born and raised in the United Kingdom, I.R. Walker moved to New York a while back. He currently divides his time between seconds, minutes, hours and days.

***

Printed in Great Britain
by Amazon